paper
aeroplanes

paper aeroplanes

DAWN O'PORTER

HOT
KEY
BOOKS

First published in Great Britain in 2013 by Hot Key Books
Northburgh House, 10 Northburgh Street, London EC1V 0AT

A CIP catalogue record for this book is available from the British Library.

ISBN: 978-1-4714-0036-0

1

Typeset by Palimpsest Book Production Limited, Falkirk, Stirlingshire
This book is typeset in 11pt Sabon

Printed and bound by Clays Ltd, St Ives Plc

Hot Key Books supports the Forest Stewardship Council (FSC), the leading
international forest certification organisation, and is committed to printing
only on Greenpeace-approved FSC-certified paper.

www.hotkeybooks.com

Hot Key Books is part of the Bonnier Publishing Group
www.bonnierpublishing.com

For Nana

Paper Aeroplanes is a novel about Renée and Flo – two teenage girls who realise pretty quickly that without each other they struggle to be themselves. It's about friendship, good and bad.

Although there are some similarities in the girls' lives (particularly Renée's) to my own, every character in this book is entirely fictional. I did however use my own teenage diaries for inspiration. The book is set in 1994, and the girls are fifteen, which is how old I was then. It's set in Guernsey – a small island just off France – and anyone local will recognise many of the places I write about, but I have changed some names to create a new world for Renée and Flo.

Reading back through my diaries from this age was as fascinating as it was excruciating. In a time where there was no Facebook, no Twitter, no mobile phones and obviously no internet, friendships worked very differently. As much as I rely on the internet more than the air I breathe, it's been fun to remember how simple everything used to be.

I hope you enjoy this story. It's been cathartic to write and brought back lots of memories. Having my own diaries as my guide to how it really feels to be a teenager has been invaluable; I just wish I hadn't stopped writing them when I was sixteen. If you are a teenager now and keep one, don't stop. Reading your own words many years later is the best story of all.

I take my place on the front bench of the science lab. A few weeks ago we had been dissecting pigs' trotters and all the vegetarians were huddled in a corner trying not to look. I thought it would be funny to flick a bit of trotter at them from the end of my ruler. As it turned out, it wasn't very funny. I only meant it as a joke but it landed inside Kerry Bowden's pencil case and she screamed like someone had run over her foot.

Vegetarians are so dramatic. What's it all about anyway? I mean, I respect animals, but I also respect the food chain, and one of the few pleasures I have living with Nana and Pop is that once a week I'm allowed to have a tin of Chicken in White Wine Sauce with a pouch of Uncle Ben's rice. I have the whole tin, in a bowl, poured on top of the rice and I sprinkle so much salt on it that not all of it dissolves. The reason I love the Chicken in White Wine Sauce so much is because Nana gives it to me while Pop is at the snooker hall on Thursdays, and she lets me eat it with a spoon sitting on the floor next to the heating vent, because that is my favourite place. That fifteen *minutes once a week is my idea of heaven. Not only does tinned Chicken in White Wine Sauce taste like the most delicious thing ever – with the possible exception of Wotsits – but Nana only has to heat it up, so even she can't ruin it.*

Nell has recently announced that she is a vegetarian. When she told Pop he shouted at me for filling her head with nonsense, and Nana cried. I think everyone in my family is actually starting to lose their minds.

Guernsey

September 1994

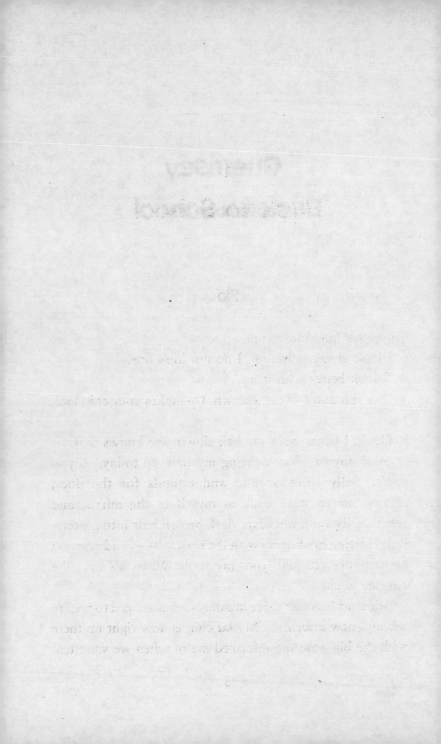

1

Back to School!

Flo

'You look fine. Hurry up.'

I look at my reflection. I do not look fine.

'I look better with it up.'

'No you don't. Wear it down. Up makes your chin look big.'

Ouch. I never wear my hair down, she knows that.

'And anyway, I'm wearing my hair up today, so you can't.' Sally spins around and pounds for the door, leaving me to stare back at myself in the mirror and rebelliously yank my limp, dark brown hair into a ponytail. Hurting my fingers with the elastic band and wincing as hairs are plucked from my skull. When it's up, all I can see is chin.

Brilliant! In under three minutes she's managed to inspire a brand-new insecurity. My fat chin is now right up there with the big nose she informed me of when we were ten.

If there was a GCSE this year in making me feel paranoid, she would get an A+.

I leave the toilets, hair down, and chase her up the corridor. She beavers her way to the classroom with all the menace of a headmistress in the making. No one wears the green school uniform quite like Sally, her shirt equally tucked in all the way around and her thick green skirt exactly at the regulation length, just on the knee. Her tie – real, unlike my fake one on an elastic band – is in the perfect knot, her light brown hair gathered on top of her head like a dog poo. She moves forward like she's on rails, her nose in its usual tilted position, her eyes searching for something to tell off, her aura oozing imminent battle. I walk alongside her, my big nose leading the way like an arrow losing speed. All summer I have told myself that this year will be different, but I'm only one morning into a new school year and my 'best friend' has me quivering in my knee-length socks.

'Why do we have to sit right at the front?' I ask nervously.

'Flo, you do this every year. I get us to school as early as I can so we can get the best desks in the classroom, and you just moan, AND you always make me late. We only just about made it before anyone else because you were faffing so much.'

'Sorry. I had to give Abi her breakfast.'

'Why doesn't your mum do that? It's her child,' Sally says, proving she's never listened to a word I've said.

'Because Mum and Julian were in the living room talking about Dad.' I dump my rucksack onto my new desk. 'Did I tell you he moved out?'

'Julian moved out? Why?' She wobbles the chair that's at her desk and swaps it for one that doesn't wobble in the row behind.

'No, *Dad* has moved out,' I say, getting annoyed but trying not to show it.

'Flo, are you going to go on about your dad being depressed again? It really brings me down.'

'He moved out, and I miss him.'

'It's all you talk about,' says Sally, meanly.

I start to arrange my desk.

'Haven't you even got a new pencil case this year?' Sally asks, moving the conversation on.

'This one is OK,' I say quietly.

'OK, OK, OK. Everything is always just "OK". It's so boring. Who wants to be "OK"?'

I sit for a moment and think about what she said. It doesn't take me long to realise that I, quite genuinely, just want to be OK.

Renée

Nana rips open the curtains and stands over us, mumbling something along the lines of 'New term, new start'. I throw my hands over my eyes to try to ignore the morning, but she is determined that this will be her first and final visit to our bedroom before school.

'I'm in the bathroom first,' barks Nell as her skinny silhouette stalks past the end of my bed. She'll be in there

5

for ages as usual, but I can wait. My hunger is already forcing me to get up.

Pop is sitting at the kitchen table wearing a white vest, gulping hot tea like a glass of water and fixing the sole of one of Nana's shoes. He is making grunting noises.

'Morning, Pop. Want some bacon?' I ask.

'I don't eat during the day,' he replies, not looking up.

I already knew that. He's never eaten during the day. Mum told me it was about control. That he sets himself challenges to remind himself who is boss. If you ask me, he doesn't need to skip meals to show anyone who is boss. With a temper like his, no one is in any doubt who makes the rules in this house.

'Make sure you make enough for your little sister, Renée. Don't be selfish.'

I loaf over to the fridge, peel four slices of value bacon from the massive pile in the packet and dangle them in front of me as I walk over to the stove. I know full well that making breakfast for Nell is a total waste of time.

'I want an egg as well. No, I want two eggs, and bacon, and three slices of toast, and cocoa pops,' she says when she comes downstairs. She shovels food into her mouth like she hasn't eaten for weeks. Nana and Pop tell her she's a good girl, but I find it hard to watch.

After washing up my plate and the cups that were left in the sink, I kiss Nana. She's holding her fixed shoe that's just two short walks away from failing her for the fiftieth and final time. I head up to the bathroom.

'You washed your plate, Renée?' Pop shouts after me.

6

I bite my tongue.

With the bathroom door closed I open Mum's make-up drawer. It's still just as she left it eight years ago. The smell of Chanel No. 5 comes wafting out. Her blusher brush still red at the tips, exactly the same colour as her cheeks used to be. I close my eyes and run it over my face. As the bristles tickle my nose all the hairs on my arm stand up and then a solid tear falls out of my eye and lands on my top lip. I don't know why some mornings I get a tear and some mornings I don't. Maybe it has something to do with my dreams. Last night I dreamed that Mum didn't really die, that she had just got into trouble with the police and had to go into hiding until they stopped looking for her. I woke in the night convinced it was true, then realised it couldn't be as I was in bed in her old bedroom, the room that she died in. The last place I ever saw her.

I love Mum's drawer. The fact that no one has thrown anything from it away is proof that we're all clinging on to something. This evidence is comforting as no one would ever say it out loud. I know the others look in it too because sometimes I lay a hair over her make-up and by the end of the day it has always moved. The drawer is like an altar in a church. It's sacred. To get rid of Mum's drawer would be the final stage of letting her go. None of us is ready to do that.

'HURRY UP!!' yells Nell as she pounds on the door. I quickly brush my teeth and let her in. She snarls at me as I skim past her and the door is slammed shut before I barely have the chance to get through it.

Five minutes later I am dressed. My school uniform at least reminds me that there is a life for me beyond this grey, depressed house. I run down the stairs, grab the sandwiches I made last night from the fridge, and leave.

The summer holidays have been long. I can't wait to get back to school.

My walk to school serves its purpose, as always. I like to call it my daily evolution. I leave the house with my head hanging and arrive at school with my chin up ready to have some fun. It's like the picture in the science lab of the ape turning into man by gradually standing up over a series of drawings. I leave the house an ape, I arrive a human. OK, maybe ape is a bit dramatic, but I really don't feel like myself when I am at home.

My teachers say in my reports that they wish I put as much effort into my schoolwork as I do messing about, but I say balls to that. They also say I should learn to keep a lower profile, but balls to that as well. I bet no one ever tells Madonna she should keep a low profile, and if they did she'd never listen.

As I walk up the path that takes me to the tennis courts and through the school's back gate, the concrete building of school slumps in front of me. Tudor Falls is an ugly building with a lovely name, but I can't help but smile when I see it. School makes me happy, in a funny kind of way. For eight hours every day I get to be myself. Well, a better version of myself than I am at home, anyway.

I run up to the entrance hall. The smell of polished wood coming from the assembly hall tickles my throat.

8

As I walk over the freshly hoovered carpet tiles the bell rings out like a screaming teacher, reminding me that I'm late. I run through the entrance hall, past the headmistress's office and the staffroom – which is already leaking out the smell of freshly puffed smoke – and towards Room Six, our new classroom for Year 11. Running in the corridors at Tudor Falls School for Girls is highly illegal, but as everyone else is already where they're supposed to be I can get away with it. I slam through the swinging double fire doors that divide the corridor into two halves, but stop dead at the sound of a violent thud.

I creep back and peek through the glass. It's Miss Le Hurray, head of history. She's on the ground and rubbing her nose – the swinging doors had swung back and pelted her right in the face. I hover for a second. I should help her, but an order mark on the first day would be bad – four mean a detention. I watch her through the glass, looking for signs of brain damage. She rolls onto her side and brings herself up to standing, then reaches a hand to the back of her head and gives it a rub. There's no blood. Assessment made, I continue to run. I have to get to registration.

As I burst into Room Six I can see that everyone has already chosen who they'll sit next to for the following year. Carla and Gem, my 'best friends', are over by the windows at the back, sitting next to each other of course, both waving frantically at me but not bothering to get up. As usual I do my best to look like I don't care, already feeling the neglect that comes with being the third wheel to an indestructible duo. I can see the only spare desk is in the second row back from the front on the right-hand side of the room. It's miles away from Carla and Gem and next to Margaret Cooper, who I've sat next to for the last five years.

I'm habitually late at the beginning of term, and Margaret always saves me a place. I like her, she's funny, but we're not really friends. We mess around in class and partner up when we need to. I never phone her at night, or hang around with her at the weekends. She is just the only other person in our year without a best friend. So when Carla and Gem get all possessive of each other and forget I even exist, I have Margaret. It's good to have a Margaret at school.

In Year 9 we did sometimes go round to each other's houses. One time her mum picked me up after netball club and we really stank so we had a shower. When I saw her naked I couldn't believe how much pubic hair she had. Mine was just a little tufty bit down the middle, but she had a massive bush. I sometimes wonder if Margaret ever thinks it's weird that I saw it, but out of everyone in the class she developed the earliest and she seems to be quite open about all that stuff. She had boobs when we were twelve, and I know she started her periods ages ago because she always has loads of panty pads in her desk and doesn't try to hide them. I find that really weird. I've never told anyone about my periods, even though I started over a year ago. I get all my panty pads by sneaking into the sick room during break times. The idea of buying them kills me.

My lateness has caused another major balls-up in the seating arrangement. The only seats Margaret has been able to get for us are directly behind Flo Parrot and Sally

Du Putron. Margaret Cooper I can handle, but sitting so close to Sally makes my skin itch.

Sally and I hate each other. We always have. It started when I came back to school after having a few days off after Mum died. She was so horrible. The headmistress had announced what had happened in assembly so that everyone knew to go easy on me when I came back to school, but Sally didn't get that hint. As soon as I walked into the classroom she came storming over to me and insisted I had made the whole thing up to get attention. After sobbing and convincing her that I had in fact lost my mum to a hideous disease that made her shrink to half her size and cough like an old man, she took another tack and told me that Mum had died because she hated me, and then insisted that I tell her what a dead body looks like. Which I couldn't do, as I was taken out of the room before it happened. I wasn't even allowed to go to the funeral, but Sally didn't care about that.

You have to be a certain kind of person to know how to be that much of a bitch at seven years old. I honestly think that Sally Du Putron is pure evil. She isn't nice to anyone, especially her best friend Flo Parrot. Who, to be fair, must be a bit of a twat to put up with it.

Flo

I don't care where we sit, it doesn't matter to me at all, but Sally is militant as always and I can't be bothered to

11

fight. I just sit where she tells me to and don't make a fuss. If I answer back she gets loud and shouty. I don't want everyone seeing how badly she pushes me around. It's best just to take it.

God knows what people must think of me – some nervous, quiet drip with no opinion probably. It wouldn't be far off the truth. I should have stood up to Sally years ago, but she'd make my life hell if I did and anyway, all I care about this year is passing my GCSEs. Good GCSEs means good A levels, and good A levels means university, which means I can get off this island. Guernsey may be beautiful, but if you want to escape your life, being on an island seven miles long and four miles wide makes things very difficult.

At 8.35 a.m. our new form teacher comes in. Sally has been arranging the stuff in her desk for about ten minutes but now the lid is down, her back is straight, and she is doing her best 'notice me' face.

'Good morning, girls. My name is Miss Anthony.'

We all stand up.

'Gooooood mooorrrrning, Miss Anthoooooonnnnnyyy.'

I don't know why it has become normal for us to greet teachers in super slow motion like this, but we always do it.

She's pretty, which is a surprise. Up until now all female teachers at Tudor Falls School for Girls have pretty much had a hump and facial hair, but Miss Anthony is beautiful. She's about thirty, slim and quite tall. Her hair is dark blonde and curly, shiny and down to her shoulders. She has a white blouse tucked into a tight knee-length skirt, and pointy shoes with a not-too-high heel. She looks gentle and kind and she smells like Rhubarb and Custards. She's the most attractive teacher we've ever had at Tudor Falls. I like her instantly.

I can see Sally's brain ticking over. She's upset by Miss Anthony's prettiness and has obviously already decided not to trust her. Her eyes scan her from head to toe, clearly longing for a form teacher with a hump, who doesn't make her feel ugly. Which I hate to say, without the nicely organised hair and impeccable uniform composition, Sally kind of is.

Renée

As Margaret and I sit and compare how corn beefy our legs are, a note hits me on the back of the head.

Renneeeeeeeeeeee
How was your summer? Can't believe we are back at school already, the holidays went so fast. As if our GCSEs are this year . . . do you still think you won't bother doing any revision? We missed you and your funny little ways. Sorry we didn't see you, you know how it gets. Are you and Lawrence together now??
Friends Forever, Carla and Gem x

13

I turn around and make a silly face at them. They laugh. I've missed them too, but I'm upset they haven't saved me a place nearer to them, and that they only phoned me once all summer to tell me what a great time they had on holiday together. I hardly went out for the whole six weeks because I had to work on a building site to pay back Paula Humphreys after I had a go on her moped at a party and rode it into a ditch. Her mum called Pop and insisted I paid the full cost of the bike back. He went nuts at me and didn't even care that it wasn't my fault because the driveway was really bumpy and it was pitch black. It's not fair, because Carla and Gem's mums give them loads of pocket money so they never have to work during the holidays. I bet they never have to get jobs.

Everything's just so nice for them, and that's pretty hard going when I have to go home to Nana and Pop every night. Their mums, their dads, their brothers and sisters, they all just get on. I don't feel normal around them and I know they think my family is weird. Especially since the time they came over and Pop yelled at them to shut the front door even though they were literally just saying goodbye. What is it about old people that means they feel the slightest draught from two rooms away? Carla and Gem both said it was fine, but it wasn't fine and I know they'll never come to mine again after that. Why would they when their dads crack jokes and their mums make amazing food? No wonder they never phone me. Pop scares everyone.

Hey
Don't worry about it, I was busy anyway. Saw
Lawrence loads. He told me he loved me a few weeks
ago so it wasn't like I was on my own. See you at
break time x x x

Miss Anthony sends me into the corridor for passing notes in class. Not a great start to the new school year. A brand-new teacher already wants me to keep a low profile. I eat a Wagon Wheel in the corridor as I wait for everyone to come out for assembly. School is just the same as ever.

Flo

Flo
I'll come to your house after school but let's sit in
the lounge with Julian instead of in the kitchen like
we usually do. That reminds me, do you want me to
steal Mum's Weight Watchers book for you?
She's picking us up. Be ready when the bell goes.
Sal x

As soon as the bell goes she's packing her bag and telling me to hurry up.

'Are you sure you want to come to my house? There's a weird atmosphere at home with Dad moving out. It's not exactly fun there right now,' I say, hoping I'll put Sally off.

15

'Your dad moved out? Hurry up, Mum will be waiting,' Sally says, as she pushes me by the elbow out of the building.

Downstairs in the car park her mum is doing just that, waiting. In her big Mercedes wearing her posh clothes and way too much make-up.

'You're taking us to Flo's, but I do want dinner later,' says Sally aggressively.

'OK, dear,' her mum replies, as dead behind the eyes as ever.

We get into the car – me shoved in the back surrounded by shopping bags and Sally in the front with her seat pushed right back.

'I've been in town all day,' said Mrs Du Putron. 'I got everything but the red shoes, because they don't have them in your size. But they have my number and will call when they come in.'

I think that sounds quite reasonable, seeing as it isn't Christmas *or* Sally's birthday and her mum has spent the day traipsing around town buying random items of clothing that she had picked out for herself the weekend before. But Sally has other ideas.

'Can't you just do a simple thing?' she huffs. 'I said if they don't have the red to get the blue with the platform in the six instead. They definitely had those because I put them aside. I'll just do it myself. Just drive, Mum.'

As soon as we walk in the front door of my house Sally's entire disposition changes. It happens every time. I call it

16

the Julian Effect. Girls forget themselves around my brother. Sally's voice gets shrill. She goes all red and shiny and her words come out in the wrong order. The weirdest part of the Julian Effect is that she wants to get physically close to me. When he walks into the room she rubs against me like a cat, and does weird things like holding one of my fingers in her hand while she twirls her hair with the other. If I sit down she sits on my knee, which always makes me uncomfortable because it's so unpleasant being that close to her.

'Did you like the summer holidays?' she blurts out as Julian comes into the kitchen.

'Did I like them?' he replies, with a patronising smirk.

Her mouth is so dry I can hear her lips move across her teeth. Her top lip is covered in tiny bobbles of sweat. I swear I can hear her heart beating. She swishes her tongue around her mouth and just as she starts her question again he grabs a bottle of Sunny Delight, slams the fridge shut and leaves the room. Within a second she is standing up looking like she's just done a cross-country run.

'Why do you ALWAYS do that?'

'What? What did I do?' I ask.

'Embarrass me in front of Julian. He is going to think I am such a dick now because of you. Why didn't you say something?'

I walk over to the cupboard, cover a slice of white bread in thick peanut butter and stuff as much of it in my mouth as I can. She stares at me with such disgust that I think she might actually be sick.

'Do you really want to be here?' I say, deliberately spitting food out of my mouth. 'Mum will be home soon and she'll probably be in one of her moods.'

She grabs her bag and heads for the door. 'This household is so fucked up.'

The front door slams.

A minute's silence is bliss. I take small bites of the bread and chew them slowly, loving the sensation of my hunger disappearing and the silence in my ears. Then BAM, Mum bursts in, pulling my four-year-old sister behind her.

'Feed her, will you, I'm knackered,' Mum says as she pulls a chair out from under the table and puts Abi on it.

I give Abi the rest of my bread and she takes it like it's the most exciting thing she's ever seen. My mother glares at me with her usual contempt. I feel unaffected by it. The feeling is mutual. She pours herself a glass of water and goes upstairs. I don't see her again until the morning.

Renée

By the end of the day it's like the summer holidays never happened, which isn't a bad thing. I know that fifteen is a perfectly acceptable age to get a job, but being stuck in a sweaty Portakabin on a building site doing admin and making endless cups of tea with a dirty kettle is not my idea of a good career move. It's so uninspiring to be spoken to like a moron by a load of men who stink of BO and eat fry-ups between meals. If you ask me, women should

18

be kept away from building sites for the sake of evolution and the human race.

As Carla and Gem watch me have a fag at the end of the school lane their endless positivity still surprises me. How come they never have anything bad to talk about? They have perfect families, their mums and dads love each other, they don't fight with their brothers and sisters and nothing ever seems to go wrong. One time I was at Carla's house having a sleepover and her younger sister came in, kissed her goodnight and said, 'I love you.' I waited for Carla to freak out, but she didn't. Apparently that is what happens every night. How weird is that?

Then of course they have each other.

Carla and Gem have never been lonely. They met at primary school when we were five and became inseparable. They're so close that over time even their mannerisms have become the same. Carla is blonde and Gem is brunette, they're both the same height and shape and they blend together like soup. Their clothes are cool, their bodies are perfect and they're always happy. Well, unless one of them breaks up with a boy, but that sadness never lasts. They just get over it, together.

'I'm going to have a party in a few weeks,' says Gem. 'Mum and Dad are going to a Lord's Taverners dinner and said I can have people over. I'm going to invite all the boys from the year above. Will you bring your boyfriend to this one, Renée? Or will you not tell him about it so you snog loads of other boys like you usually do?'

They fall into fits of giggles. I join in and let out the

19

occasional 'yeah, probably, but he isn't my boyfriend', then tell them I have to get home.

Home is around a fifteen-minute walk from school. I used to get lifts with Pop but when Nell decided to hate me the way that she does I told them I'd rather walk. Luckily Pop won't let Nell walk because he says she's too young. I'm not really sure how the one year between us makes that much difference in terms of a fifteen-minute walk to school, but I'm glad he won't let her because it means I get some time on my own. Kind of.

I see Lawrence sitting on the wall at the end of the school path. His big, blonde curly hair will be gone by the end of the week when the teachers have told him to cut it off. The boys' school, Grange College, isn't as strict as Tudor Falls, but the boys are definitely not allowed hair like that. He looks a bit like a poodle.

As I walk towards him I wonder what our headmistress, Miss Grut, would do if she saw me sitting on a wall swinging my legs in my school uniform. She'd probably scream at me to get down then give me an order mark or a detention. My next thought is how strange it is that I'm walking towards Lawrence thinking about school punishments. I used to run towards him and think about kissing.

Lawrence and I met at a party last New Year's Eve. We'd always known of each other, in the way that most people on Guernsey know of each other, but this was the first time we'd ever really spoken. I was trying to light a cigarette in the rain and doing such a bad job of it that the fag broke in half because it was so wet. He came over to me, threw his coat over both of our heads, lit a fag in his mouth and told me to take it. Half an hour later we hadn't moved and were snogging, his coat on the floor.

When we went back inside people were wishing each other a happy 1994. We'd missed midnight completely, which was annoying because it was the first year I'd been allowed to go to a party instead of watching the telly with Nana and Pop. But I couldn't really complain. Lawrence was lovely. He made me laugh all night, kissed me without trying to get his hand up my top and then walked me home.

I've never particularly fancied Lawrence. His face has small features and he's shorter than me. But from the day we met he's paid me more attention than anyone else I know, and for that reason being around him is lovely. He really likes me. He listens to me and asks me questions about home. No one else ever does that. So the fact that I don't fancy him hasn't really been a problem. Up until now.

'I've been waiting ages,' he says as he jumps down off the wall.

'Sorry. Carla and Gem were in one of their chatty moods. Anyway, how was I supposed to know you'd be waiting for me?' I say, sounding intentionally disinterested.

'I wait for you every day. It's my thing. Fag?'

I take a cigarette out of the packet and go to put it in my mouth, but he grabs it from me and puts it into his to light – another one of his 'things'.

'I missed you today,' he says, giving me a fixed and intense glare. 'I miss you every day.'

'You see me every day, you muppet! Don't be silly.'

21

'Did you miss me?'

I take a long, hard drag of my cigarette and stare back at him, my expression more sarcastic than his, which is so loving it makes me feel stupid. He's about to tell me he loves me again, I know it. I feel my insides tense up.

I drop my cigarette and press my face against his. I kiss him as hard as I can, as much of my tongue in his mouth as possible, as much pressure against his lips as I can manage without hurting him. I kiss him like this until I feel his words go back down his throat and disappear into his belly. When I am sure they have gone, I break away. I didn't enjoy it at all.

'Shall we go and get chips?' I ask, wiping my mouth.

His eyes are hungry, but not for chips. He thinks we're ready to have sex with each other. I know that's what he thinks, even if he doesn't say it out loud. But I know I'll never want it with him. I don't want him to even try it. Why did he have to ruin everything?

'Yeah, sure. Chips, that sounds good.'

We head towards the Cod's Wallop in town. I can tell from the way he's walking that he has an erection, but I pretend not to notice.

'I'm starving. I'm having batter bits too.'

'You eat like a man,' he says.

I decide to take that as a compliment.

2
Realising You Are Alone

Renée

The problem with having double maths first thing on a Friday is that I can't be bothered to do it. I know our GCSEs are only two terms away, but I find maths so boring and I refuse to believe that Pythagoras and his random theorum are going to get me anywhere in life. This is why four weeks into the winter term, at nine thirty on a grim Friday morning, I am lying on the floor in the toilets with Margaret Cooper eating my packed lunch and writing swear words on the bottom of all the sinks with a black marker pen.

'Have you done any craps yet?' asks Margaret.

After a short laughing fit I say, 'Crap isn't a swear word!'

'I think it is. Crap, boobs, balls . . . they're all swear words.'

This is why Margaret and I will never be best friends.

23

Anyone who thinks crap is a swear word is way too innocent for me.

'Craaaap!' screeches Margaret, scaring the *crap* out of me. 'I think I just heard the double doors.'

I'm always amazed by her hearing. Margaret can hear an approaching teacher at a hundred feet, which is why I rely on her for skiving lessons. Without her I would be in detentions every Wednesday. We grab the remains of our lunches and dive into the nearest cubicle. Like clockwork she sits so her feet are facing the front to look like she's on the loo, and I stand on the seat holding onto her shoulders for support. We take deep breaths and freeze.

The toilet door bursts open, but instead of the usual sound of the slow footsteps of a teacher on the prowl, it is someone running and quite obviously crying. They bolt into the cubicle next to us and wail. The sobbing is loud. Haunting. Full of pain.

Margaret looks up at me and we both mouth swear words at each other. She goes with a succession of craps, and I go with shit because the 'shhhh' part works well with a finger over my mouth to remind her to keep quiet.

I feel guilty listening to this person. This is real crying, and they don't know we're there. They have come here to escape something, to be alone, and here I am standing on a loo seat with Margaret Cooper between my thighs, hijacking their privacy. It feels wrong.

I hope that it's Sally. That something has happened to her that's made her realise how awful she is. That this is the beginning of her huge apology that will put an end to this horrible feud. Because as much as I dislike her, I would prefer not to have an enemy.

My head reaches the top of the partition between the cubicles, my foot digging deep into the palm of Margaret's hand as she shakes violently trying to get me high enough. I pull myself up and tip my nose over the edge to see which desperately unhappy girl is sobbing so violently in a cubicle all by herself.

It's Nell.

Flo

It's difficult trying to concentrate in double maths when you've been up most of the night looking after a child. I lay there for ages thinking Mum would go in and get Abi, but she didn't, so as usual it was down to me. Abi woke up at eleven, then again at two, and then for good at five, each time asking me why Daddy isn't at home any more. I feel so exhausted that I can't focus on the blackboard. I'm fifteen years old and bringing up a child. Mum doesn't seem to understand, or care, what it's doing to me.

I never have fun, not like everyone else seems to. It's either Mum getting at me at home or Sally putting me down at school. Other people seem to live so differently. It makes me feel totally unlikeable. Why would anyone want to try to have fun with me? I follow Sally around like a lost sheep because I don't have the courage to say what I want. It's force of habit now, I guess. I don't bother saying how I feel because one of them will make me feel so stupid for it. I've turned into a boring tagalong who watches everyone else have fun while I feel more unsure of myself every day. The only person I can be myself around is Dad, but being with him isn't the same any more. He's more pathetic than me at the moment.

At break time Carla and Gem invite Sally and I to a party. Sally says yes for both of us, but I really don't want to go. I've nothing to wear and I can't afford booze.

'Do you think your mum would buy me some ciders when she gets yours?' I ask, thinking that getting drunk might be the answer to all of my problems.

'Flo, you're a nightmare when you're drunk,' says Sally. 'Don't you remember puking into Mum's welly boot in the back of her car last time you had some of my ciders? It was disgusting. Face it, you're not a drinker. You're good at other things, like . . .' she tails off and pretends to squeeze a splinter out of her finger, ' . . . making sandwiches.'

My life is a disaster.

Renée

I feel so mad I almost run out of school three times today. How have we got to the point as a family where Nell is so full of pain that she sobs by herself at school and I don't have the guts to knock on the toilet door and ask her if she is OK? What kind of person does that make me?

I'm so angry that we never talk about Mum, and that Dad leaving is just a fact rather than a problem. Mum died a long, painful death that we all watched, and Dad left because he couldn't handle it. We're all supposed to hate him for that, but from where I'm standing none of us is dealing with it that much better. My family are like four stretched elastic bands about to be pinged and land so far apart that we never find each other again. Something has to give. Someone in our house has to say something.

I wish Aunty Jo was here. Aunty Jo is Mum's sister. She is so cool. When Mum died Nell and I thought we might end up living with her, but she met my Uncle Andrew and moved to London with him. If she was here she could make this better, but as it stands, it's down to me. Until now I've just stayed quiet, never hinting at how I feel for fear of upsetting somebody else, but after seeing Nell cry like that in a toilet cubicle, I know it's time to try. We have to talk about Mum. We just have to.

When the bell goes I'm out the door so fast I don't even have my coat on. I feel so wound up. I ignore Carla and Gem when they call after me because I know this will be the one time I won't be able to stop myself screaming in their faces. I need to get home before Pop and Nell, so that I can tell Nana we have to make everyone talk about Mum. If I get home after them then they will all be in separate rooms and I'll have to go around asking them to come and meet me in the kitchen, and that will never work. I can't do it over dinner because Pop eats like a wild animal and trying to make him focus on a conversation while that's going on is impossible. Timing is everything, so I could really do without Lawrence waiting for me at the end of the school lane and presuming that I have nothing better to do than smoke his bum-sucked cigarettes.

'Hey, don't you want a fag?'

I don't stop. I can't deal with him right now, I can't take the pressure he's been putting me under lately. Does he not understand anything about who I am?

'Renée, stop. I'll buy you chips?'

'I don't have time. I don't want a fag. I don't want chips.'

I want to scream 'FUCK OFF' in his face but somehow I manage to keep that in. I know I'm being crazy and that he doesn't know I'm on a mission to save my family from its group depression, but he is like a wall I have to run through, so I just keep running.

'But you always want a fag,' Lawrence shouts, sounding confused.

I feel like my heart is coming up into my face. It's a rage I've never experienced before. I could explode with liquid heat, or maybe just tears. The pressure building inside of me is loud and feels like sick, but not from my stomach, just like every part of me could throw something out.

I turn to him. His face is giving me a good idea of how mine might look. He looks shocked by whatever it is he sees in me.

'Please never presume what I want, or what I am thinking. No one knows what I want, or what I am thinking.' My voice is calm. I am being very weird.

28

For a split second we stare at each other. I feel an odd sense of relief in making that statement. My breath is broken, his face is still. I want to apologise but the words won't come. Instead I turn round and keep running home.

I grind to a halt at the kitchen door. I'm one step away from solving this problem. If I get this right then we might all be happy. Maybe Nell will stop treating me like I'm the devil, and Nana and Pop might find it within themselves to express something other than complete denial about Mum dying. All I need to do is open the door and tell Nana to sit down. And then wait for Pop and Nell, and make them sit down. And then talk. Like normal people.

I slowly open the door and step into the kitchen. Nana is standing at the stove boiling something that smells awful and my stomach churns at the thought of another one of her home-cooked diners. She turns to me and smiles. This is my moment.

'Nana, can we talk?'

She switches off the heat, wipes her hands on a tea towel and takes a seat at the table, almost robotically, like she's been expecting this. She looks old, but even if I hadn't seen pictures I would know that she had once been beautiful. Her hair is suddenly silver, and I mean silver, not grey. It shines and is perfectly arranged to look like a cauliflower on top of her head. She gets it done every Friday morning. Her face is all wrinkled and her eyes are soft and warm. I love her more in this moment than I ever have before. Her gentle voice, her soft hands. One of which

I reach for before I start to speak again.

'I think Nell is in trouble,' I say, already thinking I'm getting it all wrong.

'Don't start about your sister, Renée,' she replies, her eyes gently warning me.

'No, I'm not . . . But I think Nell needs help. I think we should all talk, about Mum, all of us, together. For Nell's sake.'

Nana looks down, rubs her right wrist with her left hand, sniffs, and looks back at me. 'That isn't something I can do. I'm sorry.' Her face looks so broken a piece could fall off.

She looks up at me, tearfully.

'Are you trying to make trouble, Renée?'

'No. Not trouble, Nana. I just want us to talk about Mum.'

Her tears fall just as Pop and Nell walk in. Pop shouts at me and calls me selfish for making Nana cry and Nana leaves the room. Nell gives me a look that is so hard, so scathing, that the very thought of trying to make her happy exhausts me. Seeing her crying that way at school had hurt me just as much, but what can I do? No one in this house wants my help. I think they're happier being sad.

Flo

Sally turns up at my house at 8 p.m. wearing red hot pants, black tights, huge black shoes with a solid

30

three-inch platform from the toe to the heel, a skin-tight ribbed vest, huge silver hoop earrings, loads of bangles, a fake fur coat, a ton of make-up and a black velvet cap. I am wearing a pair of My Little Pony pyjamas and some Bert and Ernie slippers. She struts past me and lands by the door of the living room like Naomi Campbell at the end of a catwalk.

'Is Julian here?'

'He's upstairs.'

'You should tell him to come down. I've got ciders,' she says, confidently.

'Can I have one?' I ask, already knowing the answer.

'No.'

I sigh and start to walk upstairs. She follows me, walking like a total slut on the off chance Julian might see her. When we get onto the landing a loud giggle comes from his room.

'WHAT THE HELL WAS THAT?' she squawks.

'Julian's new girlfriend.'

An hour earlier Julian had stormed into the house followed by a skinny blonde girl. She was dressed like a tart and couldn't walk properly because of her silly high heels. I'd just put Abi to bed and was lying on the sofa, and they didn't know I could see them. Julian poured them both some Sunny Delight and while she was drinking hers he put his hand up her skirt. Her face was really red and I wouldn't say she looked massively happy about it. After a few minutes he took his hand away and told her to follow him upstairs – her walk was even more wonky after that.

31

'What do you mean girlfriend? Since when does he have a girlfriend?' Sally asked, staring at his bedroom door.

'Julian has always got a girlfriend. Julian has hundreds of girlfriends.'

Sally looks relieved rather than disappointed. Obviously thinking the fact he sleeps with loads of girls means she is in with a chance, rather than that he has no respect for women and should be avoided at all costs.

'Did you bring me something to wear tonight?' I ask when we are in my bedroom.

'Oh, no, sorry I forgot,' she says, rummaging in her bag for some lipstick.

This is typical. All week I have been telling Sally how I have nothing to wear. How since Dad lost his job he can't afford to give me any money for clothes, and Mum won't either. She promised yesterday she would bring me something for the party, she promised four times. What's wrong with her?

I feel myself starting to cry so I face my wardrobe and pretend to choose an outfit. Most of the clothes in it are Mum's. Anything of mine is either part of my school uniform or just jeans and T-shirts and not the kind of stuff I can wear to one of Carla and Gem's parties. I don't even have any shoes, just my old burgundy DM boots. It's just me and Margaret Cooper who wear them now, and Margaret doesn't get invited to parties because she is so square. I guess that says a lot about how everyone feels about DM boots.

I'm hoping for an apology. An acknowledgement that

she's made me feel like crap about myself again, but obviously I don't get anything like that out of her. She just sits in front of my mirror, rearranging her cleavage.

'I'm not going. You go, I don't want to,' I say, trying to hold back the tears. I'm so sick of feeling ugly, and square, and uncool.

'Flo, if you think I am walking into a party on my own you have another thing coming. I didn't come all the way to your house for you to tell me you are not coming.'

'I really have nothing to wear. You promised me you would bring something. I've told you Dad has no money and that I don't have any clothes. Sally, do you not understand how crap everything is for me right now?'

'Why don't you just get a job?'

'I can't just get a job. In case you haven't noticed I have a mother who refuses to bring up her own child. I spent the entire summer holidays pushing swings or making dens out of bed sheets. I sleep for no more than five hours a night and wake up humming the theme tune to *Sesame Street* because I spend more time watching that than I do speaking to human beings above the age of four. I can't just get a JOB.'

She meets my outburst with a long silence. Turning back to the mirror she tosses her head, powders her nose, and breathes in deeply.

'Where's Abi now?'

'With Dad. He has her on Saturdays.'

'Well then, you have the night off babysitting duties, don't you? Get dressed. You can borrow my lipstick if that will make you feel prettier.' She twists the lid off a bottle of cider and takes a huge glug.

I hope she chokes on it.

Renée

I get to Gem's house early so I can borrow something to wear. They always let me borrow what I want, but because they're so sporty and eat healthy food I struggle to fit into most of their stuff now. Carla has massive boobs, but not big floppy ones like Margaret. Hers are firm and perfect, like everything else about Carla and Gem. I'm sure I could have the perfect figure if I didn't eat so many chips and didn't bunk off games all the time, but I don't have the willpower. You have to be a bit of a goody-goody to be that skinny.

I think I might be addicted to Wotsits. I should probably try to have three packets a day instead of five. And I should probably cut down on the chips after school too, but they taste so good and mean the cardboard dinners that Nana makes don't matter so much. Carla and Gem always laugh when I go round to their houses because I raid their mums' food cupboards, where there are always loads of crisps and chocolates. Carla and Gem hardly have any of it, which is so weird. If Nana had a food cupboard with anything other than tins I would never be out of it, but she shops and cooks like someone stuck in an air raid shelter waiting for war.

Gem has some white jeans that are a bit big for her. I'm really hoping she gives them to me, but generous as she and Carla are they're quite strict about me giving stuff back. Once I borrowed a tape from Carla and a week later her mum called our house to speak to me about it. I had to cycle round on my bike the next morning to give it back as apparently Carla had said I could only borrow it for a couple of days. I didn't understand why she couldn't just let me keep it and make another one. It was just a mix tape she made up herself. And why did her mum have to call my house for it? Sometimes I reckon mums think I'm bad news because of my family. They pretend to think I'm normal so they don't look judgemental, but they think I'm trouble and messed up because of Mum. I guess it's hard to argue that when I bunk off lessons all the time, but I don't do anyone else any harm.

Despite the tape thing I'm allowed to borrow clothes for parties, and the white jeans have quite a high waist so I can bend forward without my stretch marks showing. I wear them with a baggy black top that I bought over the summer and some platform shoes I got from Pandora, the only clothes shop on Guernsey that sells cool clothes for people under the age of twenty. Otherwise it's all about Marks and Spencer's and Next, and all their stuff is so boring. The shoes were £39.99, which is more than I have ever spent on anything, but I had some money left over from my summer job so got them with that. They have a sole of about three inches. Everyone's wearing big-soled shoes at the moment so it means I have something that

35

makes me cool without looking like a total fashion victim. Unlike Sally Du Putron, who dresses like such a try-hard.

Gem's house is amazing. You enter through two huge electric gates and the driveway is bigger than our back garden. To the right as you come through the gates is the house. It's painted white with lots of cute windows and ivy growing over most of the front. It has a stable door and there's a little bench just outside it where you can sit while you take off your shoes. It's all so perfect and pretty, and homely and warm. Inside, the rooms have real fires in them, and there are pictures of the family all over the place. I always think the house smells a bit like Christmas as there are so many flowers and plants and even candles. In comparison, Nana and Pop's house is like a hospital.

To the left of the driveway is the pool house and the pool, which is where the party is. There's a note stuck on the front door of the house saying NO ENTRY TO THE MAIN HOUSE but someone always manages to sneak in at some point. Last time Gem had a party one of the boys from the year above, Adam, snuck up into Gem's room, took off all his clothes and put all of hers on, including her underwear. He came back down and paraded around before jumping in the pool. Gem was furious at first but she ended up jumping in the pool after him and now he's her boyfriend. Everything always works out for Carla and Gem.

By nine thirty there are around twenty-five of us in the pool house and around the pool. I've had three 9.2% ciders and I'm sitting on a bench near the pool with Samuel

36

Franklin – a guy from the year above at Grange College who nearly everyone in Year 11 has got off with. He thinks that makes him a stud, but it actually makes him a bit of a joke. He's funny though, so he gets away with it. I like him, but even though his hand is full of intentions and stroking my leg, I have no plans to kiss him. Well, that is until I see Lawrence out the corner of my eye, staring at us. He looks really upset.

I should go and speak to him, explain that I don't feel the same way as he does and let him go gently. But I am drunk now, my head is spinning, and I wonder if maybe my family is right – if you ignore a problem, it will go away. So rather than do the right thing I kiss Samuel Franklin until I am sure Lawrence has gone. I hate every second of the kiss. And myself too, for being so cruel.

Flo

'Boys like it when girls touch each other,' Sally says, wrapping her arm around my shoulders and standing far too close to my face.

'Only if they're lesbians, Sally,' I say. 'I don't think just you sitting on my lap turns them on like you think it does.'

'Quick, sit back down. Here comes Owen Jones.' She pins me back to the chair and starts flirting shamelessly with Owen. I lean back and scan the room. Just opposite, with her back to us, is Renée Sargent, getting off with Samuel Franklin. I think everyone in our class has kissed him at some point, apart from me. The last person I got off with was Liam Miller. I'd fancied him for ages and he finally noticed me at a beach party last term. We were snogging and I was loving it until Sally put her face really close to ours and shouted 'HA. HA. HA' then told everyone how weird I am because I kiss with my eyes open. My eyes had not been open, I just opened them when I felt the presence of her big face. Liam never spoke to me again. Why would he? I'm just a freak who snogs with my eyes open.

'Sally, are you sure you need all six of those ciders? Just one won't get me that drunk,' I say, hoping the alcohol might have made her more generous.

'No way. Just face it, you can't take it. You are not a drinker.'

Apparently not. I wriggle out from under her.

'I need the loo,' I say as I walk away.

'Good, I can have the chair.'

I go into the pool house and pick up a bottle of white wine that no one seems to be claiming. Me? Can't drink? We'll see about that.

I can't be sure how I ended up underneath the weeping willow tree kissing Samuel Franklin, but it's definitely happening. He is licking my teeth. Is that a thing? And where has Renée Sargent gone, wasn't she . . .? I can't do any more thinking, it's making me spin. I can hear the party still going on so we can't have been here long. Even so, I can't remember how we got here, or how we have come to be kissing.

A belch flies up from my stomach and shoots out of my mouth, leaving the distinct taste of licorice.

I see Samuel recoil, but I'm too drunk to care.

'Do you want some more?' he asks.

'Some more what?'

'Sambuca?' He fills up the cap of the bottle and I down it. He has one too, and then we both have another. I've barely swallowed the second gulp before his tongue is running over my teeth again.

I burp again. He scrunches up his face but doesn't say anything. Instead he puts his hand on my boob. After a quick squeeze he moves down and starts undoing my jeans. My faculties must be down because I seem to be willing for him to go ahead. Everyone else has done it, so why not me? He undoes my zip. I can feel his hand against my skin. And then I remember.

'Oh no, stop it. I can't!' I screech, grabbing his hand and trying to push it away.

'Don't be frigid,' he says, half his mouth still inside mine.

He pushes his hand further into my pants and then yanks it out so fast he nearly takes my knickers with it. He is on his feet.

'GROSS. I can't believe you let me go in there with that going on.' He runs over to the pool and dunks his hand in like he's being attacked by a swarm of wasps. I'm still lying down under the tree, just my feet illuminated by the outside lights. The empty bottle of white wine is next to me, my jeans are undone, my limbs and head are about as useful to me as cucumbers.

'I'm sorry, I forgot,' I slur.

'How can you forget?' he says with total disgust.

'I'm not a very good drinker.'

'No shit!' He picks up his bottle of Sambuca and storms back to the pool house. After a few minutes I hear a roar of laughter. One cackle in particular makes me want to shrivel up and die under this tree. I have proved her right again.

I feel so sick. If I can just get to a bed to have a little lie down then I can sleep this off and get home later. I grapple onto all fours, then, like a sick dog trying to find somewhere to die, I follow the perimeter of the garden wall all the way to the main house. The door is open. I fall through it. This is better. I have no idea what happens next.

Renée

It's 11 p.m. I am drunk. I think I've had about six ciders and quite a few shots of Sambuca. Carla and Gem are both straddling their boyfriends on a sofa and there are loads of people round the pool smoking weed. Samuel is getting off with a girl from the year above and Lawrence is nowhere to be seen. Sally just left, she was really drunk. Just before she went she was sitting alone on the floor with make-up down her face, her eyes rolling into her head. I was watching her through the window. After a good half-hour of no one talking to her she stumbled out of the pool house and down the driveway. Just as she got to the gate she threw up in a hedge, then her mum got out of her car and ran to help her, but Sally pushed her away and climbed into the back seat. It was like watching Cruella De Vil have a nervous breakdown. People like Sally really shouldn't drink.

I'm starving. Drinking does that to me. Carla and Gem never eat when we drink, they say it's a waste of calories, but I have to. The snack cupboard is all I can think about. Maybe Gem's mum will have some of that ready-made prawn cocktail dip she gets. I need a big dollop of that between two slices of white bread and a packet of salt and vinegar Walkers, that'll sort me out. I have an excuse to go into the house because my bag is in there, so I walk boldly and with purpose so I look less suspicious.

As I walk through the entrance hall towards the kitchen I see a DM boot sticking out of the downstairs loo. I go to pick it up but realise it has a foot in it, and that there is a leg attached to the foot.

'Margaret?'

I pull the door open and expect to find her lying dead and murdered on the floor, but it isn't Margaret. It's Flo Parrot. She's passed out on the floor with her pants down, holding a tampon. Further inspection reveals a used one in the toilet. I'm no Miss Marple but I am guessing she's fallen off the loo halfway through the job. This is doing nothing for my nausea.

'Flo. FLO.' I shake her with my foot but she doesn't wake up. It's a moral dilemma. This is Sally Du Putron's

41

best friend; she's an enemy by proxy. Really I should just leave her, but she's about to make a total mess on the floor. If she does that Gem's mum might get mad for once and not let us have any more parties and besides, Flo Parrot has never actually done anything to me. She has to wake up.

'Flo. FLO.' I kneel next to her and shake her as violently as I can without risking a brain injury. She is breathing and making groany noises but is totally out of it. I try all the obvious things like splashing water in her face, running her hand under the cold tap – but then I remember that is what you do when you want a sleeping person to wet themselves so I stop quite quickly. I shout in her ear, but nothing. It's getting late, Gem's parents will be home soon and I can't just leave Flo lying here with her pants down surrounded by period paraphernalia. I flush the toilet, prize the unused tampon out of her hand, think for a moment about doing the unthinkable but instead fold a massive wedge of loo roll and put it in her pants. After a bit of yanking and pulling, she is dressed again.

'Flo, wake up . . . you can't stay here. Flo. FLO!'

I now feel totally responsible for her, which is annoying. If I leave her and she chokes on her vomit then I will have played a big part in her death. Sally has left – not that she would have tried to help Flo anyway. She'd probably have taken loads of photos and then passed them around class on Monday. I exhale loudly, for no one's benefit other than mine, and think about doing a runner, but I can't do that. Nope, this is down to me. I have to get her home.

42

I remember where she lives from a birthday party she had when we were in primary school. It's not too far away. If I can just get her to stand up I can probably walk her home. It's amazing how an experience like this can sober you up.

I get her to her feet. With one arm around my neck and her legs dragging on the ground, we're off.

'Come on, Flo. I'll get you home. Everything's going to be OK.'

It takes us three-quarters of an hour to walk just under a mile. She falls into three hedges, nearly gets run over twice, and she keeps saying 'I am not a good tinker', which I presume means she isn't a good drinker. I don't think she has a clue that it's me who's with her.

The house is bigger than I remember, a huge white town house on a main road just up from the hospital. Three cars are parked in the driveway and there's music and male voices coming from inside. I prop her up the best that I can next to me. I bang on the door.

When he opens the door I nearly drop her. He's holding a bottle of Budweiser that's half full. His dark blond hair is messy but thick and clean. His eyes are dark brown and they sparkle. His bottom lip is full with a perfect curve to his mouth that exposes some of his teeth. His nose is straight and he has a bit of a beard. He's tall, with broad shoulders. He's wearing quite baggy jeans with a black T-shirt and the top of his boxers is poking out. His chest is wide, his middle narrow, his legs are long. His fingernails are clean and his arms are the perfect amount of hairy.

He is the most handsome person I have ever seen in real life. Every detail of his body floods into my head at a million miles an hour. Who is he?

'For fuck's sake,' are his first words. 'Did you get her into this mess? Who are you?'

'Renée. No, I found her and brought her home.' I feel very small all of a sudden. Like a little mouse.

'Sure you did. Good one.' He takes her from me and we go inside. He drops her onto the couch in front of all of his friends.

'We should take her upstairs. I don't think she would like everyone seeing her like this,' I say, feeling sorry for Flo, who is looking pretty rough.

'She's my bloody sister. Who are you again?'

'Renée,' I say, trying not to stare at him too much.

'OK, well, I am going to carry her upstairs and you're going to get her into bed. Does that work for you?'

'Yes.'

'Good.'

He picks her up and throws her over his shoulder like a lumberjack moving a tree. I follow him upstairs. He's bumping her around but at least she isn't being stared at by all his mates. In her room he drops her on the bed.

'OK, over to you.'

'Thank you,' I say, as he goes to the door. 'Where does she keep her pyjamas?'

He laughs and goes downstairs.

I rummage through her drawers and find a pair of My Little Pony PJs. She probably hasn't worn them in years

44

but they will do for tonight. It isn't easy getting them on her but her clothes are filthy so I can't let her sleep in them. She barely opens her eyes as I do it. When I've finished I turn off the light and close the door.

Downstairs in the hall I nervously push open the door to the living room. All five of the boys go quiet.

'Bye then,' I say, trying to sound confident.

He looks at me as if to suggest I should only have entered with something interesting to say. I go to leave.

'Hey, Renée,' he calls after me. 'Nice jeans.'

I could die.

Flo

Sally's been a real cow this week. I don't know if she'll ever stop laughing at me about what happened Saturday night. There are only so many times you can be reminded of the most embarrassing thing that's ever happened to you. I don't think I'll ever go to another party again. Samuel is always out, I won't be able to avoid him. I'll be known as Period Pants Parrot forever. Maybe it will be all forgotten by everyone else, but there's no chance Sally will let it go. She's told everyone at Tudor Falls and I know her dream scenario would be to bump into Samuel and his mates so that she can embarrass me in front of them.

Double science on a Thursday morning is my favourite time of the entire week. Not because I'm riveted by the Periodic Table, but because I got dropped down a set, which ended up being the best thing ever. Sally is in Set One, I am in Set Two. This means I can only get a C or below in my GCSE but also that I get an hour and ten minutes of freedom away from her, which is worth the sacrifice of a Grade A.

I sit on the second row back in the science lab because the teacher, Mrs Suiter, has a tendency to hold really uncomfortable eye contact if you sit at the front. I think it's a nervous thing. When she's speaking for more than say, thirty seconds, she picks someone on the front row, locks eye contact and doesn't let it go until she turns to write something on the blackboard. I can't handle it at all. I find myself not knowing what part of her face to look at – her nose or mouth, or sometimes I just go cross-eyed trying to focus on the bit in between her eyes. Sitting on the second bench from the front is the best solution.

When Mrs Suiter turns to write something on the blackboard, something hits me on the back of the head. I look down. There's a paper aeroplane by my right foot with my name on it.

Hey
I hope you didn't feel too awful on Sunday morning?
Sorry about the My Little Pony pyjamas, I couldn't
find anything else.
Renée x

I don't move for around three minutes. What is she talking about? How does she know about my My Little Pony

46

pyjamas? I turn around to make a confused face at her. She smiles and waves. I smile too but I'm not sure why. This is very weird.

Hey Renée
Did you mean to send this to me?

I fold the piece of paper, following the lines. It doesn't quite make it to her at the back when I throw it, but she pretends to drop a pen off the front of the bench and walks around and picks it up. I'm not sure it would have crossed my mind to do that.

A few minutes later it hits me on the head again. I unfold it to see a picture of a girl with horns on her head and big, mean teeth. SALLY is written across the top. I laugh so loud that Mrs Suiter asks me what's so funny. I tell her it was a sneeze and she believes me, which makes me laugh even more because it sounded nothing like a sneeze. She doesn't think to tell me off as I hardly have a track record of messing around in class. I turn around and Renée giggles back at me. When the bell goes, she comes over to my seat.

'Do you not remember me taking you home?'

I think for a second. I remember something, something about falling into a hedge, and headlights. And someone helping me up.

'Was that you? Oh no, was I embarrassing?' I ask, bracing myself to be laughed at.

'No, just drunk. We've all been there,' Renée says, as if it was nothing.

47

We start to walk into the corridor. I don't really know what to say. This is all so bizarre. Renée Sargent was in my house? She dressed me for bed?

'I'm sorry I got off with Samuel. I hope I didn't upset you or anything,' I say, feeling guilty about that.

'Don't be silly. Samuel gets off with everyone. I really don't care.'

I look at her. Her face is so cheeky. She's smiling like the sides of her mouth are being pulled by pieces of string. I find it absolutely impossible not to smile too. Then Sally's voice comes booming down the corridor.

'Flo, hurry up. We need to get down to the pavilion for hockey training early to tell Miss Trunks you're swapping partners.'

Back to reality.

Renée

I'm currently doing everything I can to be kicked off the hockey team. Today's tactic is by simply not going to training. For months now I have been deliberately rubbish but all that seems to do is get me yelled at by Miss Trunks, who is by far the moodiest person I have ever met in my entire life, and from someone who lives with Pop THAT is saying something. She's fat, ugly, and she hates girls. Well, she hates girls who don't creep up and who are not Olympic-standard hockey players. Do they even play hockey in the Olympics?

48

Why would I want to run a around a field in the freezing cold wearing a tiny skirt and a massive pair of hideous regulation green knickers? I hate having to wear regulation green knickers, but if Miss Trunks sees we're not wearing them then she screams so loud her face goes red, and we get an order mark. I don't want to get order marks for things like not wearing massive pants. I need to save up my order marks for stuff that actually matters, like skiving lessons, being caught smoking, flicking fountain pen ink at people, and playing really funny tricks on Sally Du Putron when she isn't looking.

So today, instead of hockey training, just on the other side of the wall to the hockey field, I am sitting in a circle in an old stone Victorian bath holding hands with Margaret Cooper, Nancy Plum, Bethan Collins and Charlotte Pike. We are having a séance. I nearly asked Flo Parrot to join us, but just as I went up to her Sally ran over waving a hockey stick, and I honestly thought she was going to hit me with it. I can't see why Flo is best friends with Sally. She seems so nice, and Sally is a real tit.

'All we have to do is close our eyes, hold hands and imagine a dead person,' says Nancy, our class hippy. 'My mum told me the spirits just appear.'

'I'm a bit scared,' says Bethan in her littlest voice. 'What if they want to kill us?'

Everyone loves Bethan because she is small and has a voice like a five-year-old. She's best friends with Charlotte Pike, who is massive, but not in a fat way. She's 'big boned', or so she tells us all the time. She's quite manly, with a deep, loud voice, but she's got long black hair and big boobs.

'Don't be scared, Bethan,' she says. 'It's daylight and we are outside. If any spirits are scary then I will just sit on them and you can run away.'

We all laugh.

'Right, who we gonna call?' asks Nancy. We all yell 'Ghostbusters' in unison, then apologise to each other for being so obvious. The nice thing about these girls is that no one is remotely cool. Bad jokes happen with no piss-taking and no one cares about boys or clothes. It's very different from being with Carla and Gem. Lovely as they are, all they talk about is their boyfriends, their new clothes, the parties they go to. It all gets a bit boring. I like being girly to a point but it can all get a bit high-pitched and frilly with Carla and Gem. With this little crowd I am the cool one. I like that.

'I don't know anyone who is dead,' says Bethan.

'What about Marilyn Monroe?' suggests Charlotte.

'Do you honestly think Marilyn Monroe will come and visit us in this old stone bath in Guernsey?' Nancy snaps.

'She might. My mum says that when you die it doesn't matter who you are or what you look like any more,' says Charlotte, confidently.

'Well, we can't call Marilyn Monroe. Has anyone get any other suggestions?' Nancy says, losing her patience a little.

There are a few minutes' silence. I find myself closing my eyes and screwing my face up as if preparing to be punched. And then Margaret blurts, 'What about your mum, Renée?'

I open my eyes. All four of them are looking at me like hungry puppies.

'I'm not bothered,' are my first words. Shortly followed by, 'Sure, whatever.'

I never let on a shred of emotion about Mum at school. I pretend I don't care if I mention it at all. It's easier for me that way, because generally as soon as someone shows me sympathy I burst out crying.

'Great!' says Margaret as she grabs Bethan and Nancy's hands. Charlotte squints at me and lowers her head to find my eyes. When I look back at her she raises her eyebrows as if to ask 'Sure?'

I nod dramatically and reach for their hands. 'Let's do it! I don't believe in this nonsense anyway.'

'Calling the spirits. Spirits, are you there?' starts Nancy in a weird, breathy voice. 'Spirits, come to the bath and show us your face.'

'SHOW US YOUR FACE?' cries Margaret hysterically. 'What if they died in an accident and their face is mangled?'

'Bloody hell, have some respect, Margaret,' says Charlotte. 'Renée's mum didn't die in an accident, she died of cancer. Her face will be fine.'

This isn't true. The last time I saw my mother's face it was grey and loose, like an empty plastic bag. Her eyes looked lower than they had before. Her cheekbones stuck out like hard lumps that were hurting her from the inside.

51

Her face wasn't fine at all. I don't want to see it again, not like that.

'Oh yes, sorry. I forgot we were calling your mum. Maybe you should ask her to come on her own, Nancy? We might get all sorts turning up if you just say spirits,' says Charlotte, taking control.

'OK, good idea. What was your mum's name, Renée?' asks Nancy, with no sense of awkwardness about using the word *was*.

'Helen,' I say, my eyes still closed. My head is telling me not to believe in this, but I still find myself imagining her face. What if she comes? What would I say?

'Right then, Helen it is. OK, everyone hold hands again.' Nancy gets herself back into the zone and tries again. 'Helen, are you there, Helen?'

My mind starts to wander – back to when I didn't even know she was dying. The warmth of Margaret and Bethan's hands feels so nice in the cold air, the distant sound of the hockey game turns into a low hum. I start to visualise her. I can smell her, the best smell in the world – Chanel No. 5, cigarettes and leather. The perfect smell.

I go back to when I must have been all of five, still having afternoon naps but old enough to have them on the sofa and not in my room. Was that normal? I'm not sure. I woke up to see her face at the living-room door. Her black hair in loose waves sitting just above her shoulders, her nose red from the outside cold, her long eyelashes bold and upright. They surrounded her massive brown eyes like the over-pronounced sun rays I used to draw that Mum would stick on the fridge. As I woke up from my sleep she came over, took off her fur coat and crawled onto the sofa with me. She scooped me up into her arms and put her cheek on top of mine. 'How's my girl?'

I turned around and buried my face into her neck. We lay there cuddling while I woke up properly. She yawned, and even when I was ready to move I lay there and let her dose. 'I love you, Mummy,' I said.

'I love you too, darling.'

'OH MY GOOODDD!'

Mum vanishes as the sound of Nancy's voice makes us all jump.

'OH MY GOD, did anyone else see that?' Nancy shouts, out of breath.

'Keep your voice down,' orders Charlotte. 'Miss Trunks is only behind that wall.' A loud whistle sounds as the hockey is called to a close.

'Seriously. WHO. ELSE. SAW. THAT?' Nancy is standing now. White as a sheet. 'Renée, your mum. She died of cancer, right?'

'YES,' says Margaret.

'And her ashes are spread on Herm, right?'

'YES,' repeats Margaret. I would answer the questions myself but she is getting the answers right so I guess I don't need to bother. Mum died after getting breast cancer for the second time, and Nana and Pop spread her ashes on a small island just off Guernsey called Herm because she loved it there so much. I wasn't allowed to go.

53

'Well, I just saw a crab floating over an island,' Nancy says, panting.

'You saw what?' I ask, thinking she has finally lost the plot.

'Think about it. Crabs are the symbol for cancer, and your mum is scattered on Herm. Crab over island? She is here, Renée. She is TRYING TO SPEAK TO ME.'

Nancy is the kind of person who could find something spiritual in a sausage roll. As if Mum would appear to us as a crab flapping its claws over an island. I still find myself unable to ask her to shut up.

The bell rings.

The girls get up and leave. There's a hum of chatter as they walk away.

'No way, did she come? Did we actually make a dead person come?'

None of them seems to notice that I have stayed where I am. I know I'll get an order mark for missing French, but this one will be worth it.

Flo

I thought I was OK after Rebecca Stephens, my new hockey partner, thwacked me around the face with her hockey stick. But halfway through French I thought I was going to pass out from how much my head was spinning. I went to the sick room and when I felt better I told Miss Trunks

54

I'd called my dad from the payphone in the foyer and that he was waiting outside. He wasn't really.

It's all Sally's fault. Rebecca is rubbish at hockey, she has the coordination of a drunk person. She usually goes with Charlotte Pike but Charlotte wasn't in hockey training because she has period pains, so when Sally said she didn't want to go with me any more Miss Trunks put me with Rebecca and used Sally for all the demonstrations. Charlotte is really good at hockey, probably because she's big boned. I realised pretty quickly that part of her talent is dodging Rebecca's stick – that's a skill in itself. When Rebecca hit me I thought my brain had exploded. I don't remember much about it, but I do remember Sally laughing and saying she could see my regulation green knickers when I was lying on the floor.

As I leave school, Renée Sargent is coming in.

'What happened to you? Did Sally do that?' she asks, referring to the big red lump on my forehead.

Do people think Sally beats me up?

'No, I was partners with Rebecca in hockey. Turns out she isn't very good at hockey.'

'It looks really sore. Is someone picking you up?' Renée asks, obviously concerned.

'No,' I lied. 'I'm going to walk to my dad's, he isn't feeling that great.' I notice that Renée's eyes look red. 'Are you OK?' I ask.

'Yeah, I'm fine. My eyes just get puffy when it's cold.'

We stand awkwardly for a few seconds. Eventually I

say, 'Cool, well, Miss Trunks will tell me off if she sees me. I'd better go.'

Renée looks weird. Kind of sad.

'Can I walk with you?' she asks quietly.

I look up at the French class window. Sally isn't watching.

'Yeah, I guess so.'

Renée and I walk separately until we get to the end of the school path and totally out of sight. When she catches up with me I feel so conspicuous. Bunking school and cavorting with the enemy? This is the baddest I have ever been.

'Wanna go get chips?' she says, her eyes still puffy.

I am about to say no, but I haven't had chips in ages. 'OK,' I say. 'Why not.'

'Come on then.'

We walk to the Cod's Wallop and order two portions of chips with loads of salt and vinegar. Renée starts to eat hers as we step outside.

'What are you doing?' I say. 'We can't eat in public in school uniform. If someone sees us we will get into trouble.'

'That's stupid. We're hungry, they can't stop us eating,' Renée mumbles with her mouth full.

'Can't we just go somewhere out of sight?' Once I was caught drinking a can of Coke in town and Miss Grut called my mum to say I had been seen 'hanging off the end of a Coke can' in my uniform. Mum was so mad at me for having the headmistress call home.

Renée sighs but wraps up her chips again and says she knows a field nearby. We walk there and sit under a big tree behind a hedge. No one can see us.

'So what's up with your dad?' she asks boldly.

'Oh, it's really boring. You don't want to know.'

'Yeah I do,' she insists.

'Really?'

She nods, her mouth completely full.

'OK, well, he lost his job nearly a year ago and hasn't found one since. My mum just kicked him out because he's drinking too much and . . .' I suddenly feel very uncomfortable. 'I shouldn't really be telling you this.'

'Families are idiots.'

I don't know what to say to that.

'I need to go and talk to him.' I eat a chip, and feel an unfamiliar impulse to keep talking. 'It feels a bit like I'm the only one who says anything at the moment. Mum and I don't really get on.'

'Talking in my family doesn't happen,' says Renée. 'The trick for me is to live on the edge and never tip over. It's a right laugh.'

'What's funny about that?'

'Nothing. That's why it's funny. It's so bad I just think it's funny,' Renée says, tilting her head back so the chips don't fall out of her mouth.

'Do you really?'

'If I don't laugh about it what else will I do?'

She doesn't actually laugh though. She falls back, throws chips into the air and tries to catch them in her mouth.

She misses them all but picks them off the grass and eats them anyway.

'So what about your brother?' she asks as she chews.

'What about my brother? You don't fancy him as well, do you?' I blurt, embarrassed by my defensiveness.

'What? No way! Why would I fancy him?' Renée replies, obviously offended.

'Everyone fancies Julian. Sally is obsessed with him. Sometimes I think it's the only reason she's friends with me.'

'Well, Sally is an idiot, and I do not fancy your brother. He's way too skinny, and beards are gross. I could never kiss someone with a beard.' She stuffs her mouth full of chips again, probably to stop herself slagging off my brother any more.

I don't like it when she calls Sally an idiot. Not because I don't agree, but because going behind Sally's back frightens me. If she finds out I skived school with Renée she'll make my life hell, and come to think of it, what am I doing bunking school? Sure, I have a lump the size of one of Miss Trunks' boobs on my forehead but how am I going to pass my GCSEs if I skip lessons? The rebel inside me is short lived.

'I need to go.' I reach down to pick up my bag.

'OK, well, do you want to meet up after school tomorrow?' Renée asks, as if that would be completely normal.

I shake my head. 'We have clarinet on Thursdays.'

'Ooo, well, I wouldn't want to get in the way of you

and your boss playing the clarinet,' she says under her breath, with a little smirk. It makes me feel so small. I stare at her for a while, half expecting an apology.

'No offence, but you barely make it to lessons, let alone anything extra-curricular. What do you actually do, anyway? Is this it? Chips in fields?' I am surprised at how easy I find it to answer back to her. Building up to speaking to Sally like this takes weeks of preparation, and then I usually chicken out.

'So what if it is? Where's honking down a piece of wood going to get you in life?'

'That's not the point. You learn things to make life more interesting.'

'You think playing the clarinet is interesting?' Renée says, annoyingly making me question why I do play the clarinet.

'I think it gives my brain something to think about, gives me something to focus on. What do you focus on?'

'I dunno. Fun?'

I watch her throwing chips into the air and into her mouth again. She won't look at me now. She's pretending this conversation isn't happening.

I start to walk away, but then turn back. 'You know there's more to life than skiving class and being the joker, Renée. Don't you care about the future?'

'What's the point in worrying about the future? Who says there will even be a future? What happens if you die tomorrow and all you ever did was sit in maths classes and play the clarinet and moan about your family? What good is the future to you then?' She sits up and lights a cigarette. 'Have fun at your dad's.'

'Fun . . .?' I think better of keeping this conversation going and leave her alone, sitting in the field smoking and eating chips. I get the impression she'll be there for a while.

As I get to Dad's house I can hear the TV. He's watching *Countdown*. The house is so small – barely a house really, more a little bungalow surrounded by overgrown weeds with his banged-up old Ford Fiesta in the drive. It's the car he bought Julian for his seventeenth birthday, but now he uses it because he can't afford another one. I remember when he gave it to Julian. Julian said he wouldn't drive it because it was such a 'heap of shit'.

The bungalow is a yellowy colour and the windows are filthy. It's depressing to look at. I hate that this is where he lives now. Our house is big and lovely, and although I know it's just a matter of time before we have to move out because no one can afford to pay the mortgage, it should be his house too. He bought it. Not her.

'Dad?' I let myself in with my key. The house smells of burnt food.

There's no answer.

I go into the sitting room and see him asleep in an armchair. There's an empty pint glass on the table in front of him with white froth stuck to its inside. A microwave macaroni cheese is half eaten on the coffee table, still in the plastic.

I stand in the doorway staring at my dad. His large

belly is flopped to one side, his double chin squashed into his chest. His dark blond hair that used to be combed neatly is now unwashed and too long, and his face is badly shaven, covered in cuts. He's wearing a blue T-shirt with jeans, and socks with slippers that he's obviously been wearing outside. Wearing my slippers outside was one of the only things he ever used to tell me off for. It really upset him. Thinking about that upsets me now. Dad has changed so much in such a short space of time. It feels like only yesterday he was coming into my room every morning singing stupid songs to wake me up for school. I miss it.

'Dad.' I shake him gently. 'Dad, wake up.'

He opens his eyes. No other part of him moves for a few seconds. It's creepy, like he's waiting for something to happen before he's willing to look at who woke him up. Then he sees me.

'Flo. Hello, darling,' he says sleepily, like he's been drugged or something. He shifts in his chair and tries to get up. 'Here, sit here in my chair. Do you want a cup of tea?' He starts to clear the table, making all sorts of excuses for not having done it earlier.

'It's OK, Dad. Just sit down.' I perch on the arm of the sofa and he slumps down like a child who has been told off. There are a few minutes where we both pretend to find a word in AHOGWUSPE.

'Sorry, Flo. I'll get myself back on track, I promise. And I'm sure your mum and I will work things out.'

'It's OK, Dad, honestly.'

61

'How's school? That Sally still acting like she rules the world?' he asks with a small smile.

My dad knows all about Sally and her ways. He's the one person I can tell the truth to. He seems to understand it completely. When he lived at home he came up to my room every day after work and insisted I told him all the mean things she had done that day. He somehow made it all seem funny. I'd tell him what she'd said and he'd mimic her in a silly voice that was weirdly accurate. It always made me laugh.

'Yeah, she's like a fly trap and I'm a stupid, dopey blue bottle that hovered around so long I got stuck. Makes me feel like such a loser,' I say, crossing my arms and slumping.

'Hey, it's me you're talking to. King of the blue bottles. I'm the loser.'

'Don't say stuff like that, Dad. You're not a loser.'

We look back at the TV screen. One guy has a five-letter word, the other seven.

'How is she, your mum? When she drops Abi off she barely looks at me. Can't blame her, I guess.'

'She's angry all the time. She hates having to work, and she hates having to look after Abi when she gets home, so she doesn't, I do it. I don't remember the last time I actually had a conversation with her,' I say, flitting my eyes between him and the TV.

'Nor do I, and we've been married for twenty years.'

We let out little laughs, but they don't last long.

'I miss you, Dad. Julian, Mum and Sally do my head in so badly.'

'Well, people who acknowledge their faults aren't so angry about them. Oh to be a selfish, eh?'

'I think life would be easier if I was a selfish.'

'No, it wouldn't. Not really. Those people aren't happy, they'll be on their death beds with little more than a lifetime of guilt and regret to think about. People like us die with a clear conscience, Flo. That's the best way to be. If you admit to where you go wrong at least you stand a chance of making it better.'

I still wish I was selfish.

The guy with seven letters lost. Pogwash isn't a real word.

Renée

I can't sleep. Just before bed Nell told me that she hates living with Nana and Pop and that she plans to tell them that soon. She said she doesn't care if it hurts them and that she can't live like this any more. When I asked her where she plans to live instead she said 'with Dad'. If she ever says that to Pop I think he would explode, and Nana would cry, and things would only get worse.

Dad made his decision to live in Spain. When Mum died him and Pop had the worst fight. I'll never forget how loud they shouted at each other. Pop said it was his fault she got cancer, that the stress he put her under is what made her ill. I don't think that's true, I think Pop just needs someone to blame because his daughter died before he did and his brain can't handle it. He turns everything into a battle, and has to make everything somebody else's fault. Sometimes I wonder if he really blames himself. He made Mum, after all. Maybe he feels responsible for her body going wrong. Maybe that's why he's so mad all the time, and why he shouts and makes everyone else feel so terrible about themselves. He's trying to make us all feel as guilty as he does. I think it worked on Dad, because soon after Mum died he moved to Spain, and now he has another wife and another child. The only contact I have with him are the birthday and Christmas cards he sends, which his new wife so obviously writes. I've never even met her.

If Nell tells Nana and Pop she doesn't want to live here any more we won't be allowed to move to Spain anyway. And even if we are, I don't want to live in another country with someone who doesn't love me enough to write their own cards. And I don't want to start all over again with a new school where no one knows me. So Nell will go and it will just be me, Nana and Pop left here. Pop will be angrier and he'll make me feel even more guilty about not being the one who died instead of Mum. And they'll get older and older and I'll have to start taking care of them, and I'll have to leave school to become a full-time carer and my life will be awful. Why can't Nell just shut up and deal with it? It doesn't make sense that I'm the one who always gets called selfish in this house.

As I lie in bed thinking all of this over I can't think of a single positive outcome of her saying that stuff. I just lie there, my heart jumping around in my chest, desperately trying to think of something, of something shallow and shiny to focus on to distract my thoughts, and then I remember.

Julian.

I listen to Nell's breathing. It's long and slow. She's definitely asleep. I slide my hand down slowly. My duvet is suddenly very loud. On my back with my hand in place, I think about him. The curve of his top lip pressing against mine, his breath bitter but sweet. We're in the living room, where I saw him last. He has me on the sofa. His hand is where mine is now, he's kissing me and touching me and he feels so good. I'm totally transfixed by my fantasy, I must unknowingly jolt, make a noise, I don't know – but Nell is now awake. She's turned the light on, and she is telling me I am disgusting.

I don't bother saying anything. It won't make me feel any less humiliated to stand up for myself. I just roll over. She turns off the light and says, 'You should always be alone, Renée.'

I fall asleep, my brain finally realising that being awake isn't worth the hassle.

The next morning I wake up to hysteria. Nana is next to Nell's bed with a bowl of water and a cloth. Nell is lying on her back with a tea towel stuffed up her nose. This has become normal. Nell's nosebleeds are an everyday occurrence since she decided to torture herself by not eating. I go to get out of bed, knowing that offering my help will only get me told to GO AWAY, but as I move I feel a wetness between my legs that worries me. Is it already that time? I lift the covers and see that my pyjamas have a huge red stain creeping across them. I move myself to see if it had spread to the sheets but I've woken up just in time. Any wrong move will change that so I have to be careful. I roll onto my side and run to the bathroom. Pulling my PJs down as I go I just about make it to the toilet, but a dollop of blood falls onto the mat.

Why do periods have to start that way? This will be my fifteenth and I'm still not used to them. I can't believe I have to have them until I'm fifty-something. How many pairs of pyjamas will I have ruined by then?

I clean myself up and stick a big wedge of loo roll between my legs. Holding it in place with my thighs I scrub the toilet mat until the stain comes off. After a shower I hold my pyjama bottoms between my thighs, wrap a towel around myself and waddle into the bedroom. Luckily I have one more sanitary towel in my gym bag, so I stick that in my pants, get dressed, hide the pyjamas in my bag and leave for school. Just at the end of our road there's a row of bins. I throw my pyjama bottoms into the emptiest one and carry on along my way. As I walk, I think how weird it is that Nana has never even asked me if my periods have started. Maybe when you get that old you just forget about them.

At school, hell strikes. My tummy throbs like a wild animal trapped inside a cage. I sit on the toilet as I try to push out the pain. The registration bell rings, I crawl back to the classroom. My face can't hide what I'm going through.

'Get on your knees and put your head on the floor,' insists Margaret, who is the self-confessed Queen of Periods, seeing as she started so long ago.

'NO, don't scrunch up. You lie on your back with your knees apart and feet together,' says Charlotte as she tries to get me into that position.

'I am not lying on the floor in my school skirt with my legs open,' I say, jamming my thighs shut.

I assume Margaret's position and continue to drop beads of sweat into the carpet tiles. Last month I didn't get any pain at all – why now? I feel so faint. The dull ache is weakening me. With my forehead on the floor I shout, 'Why did Mother Nature do this to us?' I take some long, deep breaths.

'Ahhh, babe. You'll be OK. It's OK,' repeat Carla and Gem. The urge to scream 'DO I LOOK OK, YOU PAIR OF PERFECTS?' at them is almost impossible to control. I pant it out, by instruction of Charlotte. Then I feel a threatening presence hovering over me.

'Why are you always trying to get attention? Periods aren't that painful.' It's Sally, her feet close to my head. 'Attention is all you care about, isn't it? Maybe if you cared about school and did some work then you'd get attention for being clever rather than a thick show-off.'

I try to ignore her, but I'm not in the most pleasant of moods.

'A school full of girls and I've never seen anyone else with their head on the floor at the back of a classroom because of a little period pain. Only you, Renée.'

Focus on the breath, focus on the breath.

I look up. Her smirking face is looking down at me. Flo is sitting at her desk pretending to read a book. It's upside down. Being beneath Sally, no matter what the reason, is not something I'm comfortable with. She steps closer to me and kneels down.

'Poor Renée,' she whispers. 'No one loves you. No friends, a mad family. It's hardly a wonder, really.'

I feel a power surge in my belly. My muscles are tightening around the pain. One swift thrust up with my head and I'll probably remove one of her teeth. I inhale deeply, ready to throw my head back and remove the smirk right from her face. One, two, thr—

'Good morning, ladies. What is all this?'

Sally jumps up. Miss Anthony is now standing over me.

'Renée, is there any particular reason you are on the floor?' Miss Anthony asks with an assertive tone.

'Period pain, miss,' offers Margaret.

'Oh dear. Well, you shouldn't be on the floor. Come on, Renée, up to your feet. Do you think you can make it to the sick room to lie down? There's a hot water bottle there. It will pass in a little while if you just lie still,' Miss Anthony says, helping me up.

'WITH YOUR LEGS OPEN,' shouts Charlotte from across the room.

'Just a water bottle will do fine, thank you, Charlotte.

Do you think you can make it downstairs on your own or would you like someone to go with you?'

I nod, embarrassed that everyone in Year 11 now knows I have my period. I hold onto the wall the whole way.

Inside the sick room both bunk beds are empty. Good, there's nothing worse than having to share the sick room. I always regret skiving when I have to lie there pretending to be ill with someone puking into a bowl underneath me. I lie down on the bottom bunk and wait for whichever member of staff is on duty to come and make me a hot water bottle. My tummy is already feeling a little better.

After ten minutes no one has come and I start to feel anxious. I need to change my panty pad. Knowing that the middle drawer in the office just off the sick room is full of them, I get up and creep in. This is where I've been getting them ever since I started my periods over a year ago. As I stuff as many as I can into my waistband, my bra and even a couple in my socks, I hear the door open.

Oh, SHIT!

'What on earth are you doing stuffing sanitary towels into your bra, Miss Sargent?'

It's Miss Trunks. She is taking up the entire doorframe. Even if I had wanted to escape I couldn't have. She looks angry, but equally as pleased to have caught me. Catching people break school rules is why I think Miss Trunks became a teacher.

'Stealing school property is a serious crime. Put those back. NOW,' Miss Trunks says, spitting all over the place.

I start to unload my bra and waistband. Of all the things to get caught stealing, at least good stationery has some level of kudos.

'So what is this about? I suppose you sell these for money to buy cigarettes, don't you?'

'No, Miss Trunks. I just needed some.'

'Don't you lie to me, Renée Sargent. A girl of your age can buy her own protection. No one steals sanitary towels unless it is to sell them to make money to spend on things like cigarettes or alcohol. Is that why you never come to hockey training? Drink? Hurry up and put those back. We're going to see Miss Grut,' she screams, winding herself up into a melodramatic frenzy.

She leads me down the corridor, pushing my elbow like a gear stick. I sit outside and wait for half an hour. Then the unthinkable happens. Pop walks in.

We sit in silence in Miss Grut's office. Miss Grut, Miss Trunks, Miss Anthony, Pop and me. Pop and I sit on two separate chairs in front of Miss Grut's massive desk. Miss Trunks, who is wearing over-stretched sports gear, and Miss Anthony, who is in a pretty high-necked flowery dress, share a two-seater sofa to the right of us. Miss Anthony looks a bit squashed.

'Renée has been caught stealing school property. Sanitary towels. The *school's* sanitary towels,' says Miss Trunks to break the silence.

'Yes, Miss Trunks,' says Miss Grut, 'we all know why we are here, thank you. And thank you for coming in so

70

promptly, Mr Fletcher. Renée, have you been stealing from the school?'

It feels strange being asked a question directly by the headmistress. She doesn't have much to do with us on a one-to-one level. She's a bit like the Queen. Everyone stands up when she walks in or leaves a room, and if you see her walking towards you in the corridor the natural reaction is to stand still until she has passed. Being asked a question by her feels part privilege, part the scariest thing I have ever experienced. Pop is sitting next to me breathing really loudly, and there's a giant pile of panty pads on her desk, deliberately positioned by Miss Trunks to remind us why we are all there.

'Not stealing, miss, borrowing.' I don't know why I say this. I obviously was stealing them.

'Why were you in the sick room?' asks Miss Grut, trying to piece the story together.

'I sent her down there,' says Miss Anthony. 'Renée had terrible cramps this morning.'

Pop shuffles uncomfortably in his chair.

'I sent her to the sick room to lie down with a hot water bottle,' Miss Anthony continues.

'And THAT is when I found her stuffing her bra with the *school's* Always Ultra,' barks Miss Trunks.

'That is quite enough, Miss Trunks. We can take this from here. Thank you for bringing this to my attention.' Miss Grut's eyes fix hard on the door. The horrible fat cow leaves.

'Mr Fletcher,' continues Miss Grut. 'Do you know why

71

Renée might feel the need to steal sanitary equipment from the school?'

Sanitary *equipment*? Adults are so weird sometimes. A minute's silence nearly deafens me. I stare at the pen pot on Miss Grut's desk to distract myself from how hideously mortified I am.

'Well, Renée is a girl, isn't she?' Pop rubs his nose and does a fake cough.

'She is, yes,' agrees Miss Anthony.

'Well, then. Girls need them things for stuff I don't know about, but you know more than me, I'm sure.'

Never have I wanted the earth to swallow me up so much. Pop trying to explain what I might use a panty pad for is as bad as the time I farted when I sneezed during prayers in assembly. At least that was funny. There is nothing funny about this. Through pure fear of him being asked to elaborate, I start to speak.

'I know it sounds stupid but I'm too embarrassed to buy them in shops, Miss Grut. So every few months I go into the sick room and take what I need because . . .' I mumble, '. . . I don't like strangers knowing I have my . . .'

'Period,' offers Miss Anthony.

'Yes, that.' I nod.

'Periods are nothing to be ashamed of, Renée. You are a woman,' says Miss Grut.

If one more person says the word period or panty pad in front of Pop I am going to have to jump out of the window, run to the sea and swim to France.

'Look, I don't steal stuff usually, it's just those.' I point

72

at the pile of pads on her desk. 'I'm sorry, I won't do it again.'

'Well, your regret seems genuine, so we're done here,' says Miss Grut. 'Mr Fletcher, maybe Mrs Fletcher can help Renée in the shop next time she has a period?' I wince, but Miss Grut continues. 'I'm sure your situation makes all sorts of conversations very hard, but as Renée turns into a woman she'll need your help on matters like this. Renée, I will let this go this time, but please don't let us catch you doing this again. Thank you, everybody.'

Pop and I are up and out the door as quickly as we can. I walk him to the foyer.

'Pop. I'm really sorry,' I say, so embarrassed I can barely get my words out.

'I will speak to your grandmother and she will take this from here. Don't be late for dinner.' Pop makes it very clear that the subject is closed. As I watch him walk away I feel like I don't know him at all. He's just a stranger who knows I am on my period.

I feel a hand on my shoulder.

'Renée?' It's Miss Anthony. 'I used to be the same when I was your age. Here.' She hands me a cotton pouch. 'Have these. Do try to build the confidence to buy your own, but this should get you through this month.' She smiles. 'Now take a minute to get yourself together and then get to class. You can still make the last half-hour of drama and I'll make sure you don't get an order mark.'

'Thank you. That's really nice of you.' I start to walk away, but Miss Anthony puts a hand on my arm.

'Renée, I lost my mother when I was young, too. I know how lonely it can feel.'

'I'm not lonely, Miss Anthony. I have lots of friends,' I answer defensively.

'Are they good friends? People you can talk to? It's really important to talk about how you feel.'

'Of course.' I nod. 'Best friends. We talk about it all the time.'

'Good, good. I am glad,' she says, looking pleased.

Later, in the afternoon, Miss Grut comes into our French class unexpectedly. Everyone stands up, but she tells us to sit straight down. Assuming she has changed her mind and is here to punish me for theft I start to pack up my pencil case, but instead she walks over to Flo Parrot and asks her to follow her downstairs.

I have only ever seen that happen once at school before. When I was seven years old.

3

When the Worst Thing Happens

Renée

I wake up feeling strange. This November has been particularly glum. I've got soaked on the way to school most mornings, but still I choose to walk instead of getting a lift with Pop and Nell. I often wonder, are things so uncomfortable between us that I should really have to deal with wet socks for most of the day at school? And I always conclude yes. Besides, despite watching me take the sandwiches I have made out of the fridge every morning (I've made my own lunch ever since I opened my lunch box one day to discover Nana had made me baked bean sandwiches) no one ever suggests I should get in the car. I am independent from this home. I live here and get involved in the necessary elements of cohabiting – eating, using the bathroom, watching the occasional TV show – but apart from that it is them, and me. I can never be quite sure how or why this has happened. I certainly didn't mean it to. I am so pleased I have Mum's drawer to keep me going, but today I find myself struggling more than usual to close it.

I don't believe in God, and I don't believe in heaven, but I can't believe that she is gone. It would be easier if when people die we are able to forget about them, but it doesn't seem to work that way. What I find hardest is that my memories are getting fuzzier, but not so distant that I can let them go. I'm sure I used to remember the sound of her voice, but now I can't. I just see her in my head, but there's no sound any more when I close my eyes. My dreams have become unreliable too.

I've been having a reoccurring dream. In it I'm sitting at the kitchen table watching Pop eat a raw steak with his hands. Nana is standing in the hallway hiding behind the kitchen door. Something calls me out to the garden. I don't know what it is – a noise, a light – it's never very clear. When I get into the garden there's a navy-blue pram and the sun is beaming directly into it. I walk over but I'm too little to see in so I have to pull myself up and get on tiptoes to peep over the side. Lying in the pram is a baby, but the baby has my mum's face. She smiles at me but can't reach out to me because she has little baby arms. I can't pick her up because I'm so small myself. So I just watch her face smiling at me, in the pram, with her baby's body wriggling around. I rarely wake up from this dream without feeling strange. I guess that's understandable.

I run her blusher brush over my face, and then, with a small spring in my step at the thought of not spending the day with water in my shoes because it isn't raining, I leave for school.

Late as usual, I arrive minutes before Miss Anthony comes in for registration. There's an unusual silence coming from Room Six. When I walk in no one is at their desks. They are all huddled around like children listening to a story. In the middle is Sally Du Putron, standing on her desk.

'They *say* it was a heart attack. I saw him last week. He was so fat and he looked drunk. I called Flo last night and her brother answered the phone. *He* told me everything.'

'What exactly did he tell you?' asked Margaret.

'He told me their dad had died of a heart attack, dip shit!' Sally says, sounding proud of her knowledge.

'Did you speak to Flo?' asks Charlotte.

'Of course I spoke to Flo, I'm her best friend! She couldn't stop crying so it was hard to make out what she was saying. That got a bit annoying so I didn't stay on the phone long, but what I did get out of her is that he was found dead in his front garden and he was wearing his slippers. How weird is that?'

I stand at the door listening to Sally. Poor Flo. Poor, poor Flo. Her poor dad. It's so sad. What happened after Miss Grut took her out of the room? Where had she first heard that her dad had died? Who was with her? I know very little about Flo Parrot, but I know that she loves her dad. I only knew Mum for seven years and I still think about her every day. Flo has known her dad for fifteen years – how could you ever forget someone you have known for fifteen years? Maybe I'm lucky.

'What the hell are *you* crying for?' Sally says, looking over to where I am standing.

All eyes are on me. I didn't realise I was crying.

'Ahhh, poor Renée, not getting all the attention this morning so she stands in the doorway and cries. BOO HOO.'

'Shut up, Sally. What happened to Flo's dad is really sad,' I say, wiping my cheeks.

'Of course it is SAD, you idiot. Flo was crying like a baby on the phone last night. She was doing that weird thing where she couldn't get her words out properly, all sniffing and hiccupping and stuff. I should know if it is sad or not. I'm her best friend, not YOU.' She glares at me then turns back to her crowd. 'So yeah, he was wearing his slippers. Outside. Don't you think that just sounds like he had totally given up on himself? I wouldn't be at all surprised if we find out he . . .' she puts her hands either side of her mouth and whispers, '*killed himself.*'

'For fuck's sake, Sally. Have some respect, will you?' I shout as I move towards her.

Her head turns slowly to look at me. The crowd disperses awkwardly. There is a general hum, suggesting that I have overstepped the mark. I swallow hard.

'Some respect. Me? With *respect*, Renée, are YOU a likely candidate for head girl? Have YOU had a tidiness

78

sash for three years straight? Have YOU ever had an A*
or never even had a single order mark? Have you got
any respect for anyone when you piss around in class
distracting us all from lessons? With *no* due respect,
Renée, the only thing you have any respect for is thinking
you are IT.'

Limbs fly everywhere as I drag her to the floor. At first
I am on top, pulling at her uniform, trying to win the fight
without actually hitting her because despite my brazen
move I can't bear the idea of whacking another human in
the face. I wrestle like a dog playing, all teeth and thumping
paws but no claws. And then she punches me. Right in
the eye. It really hurts.

'Sally Du Putron, what on earth are you doing?'

Miss Anthony is standing over us. Her timing is impeccable.

'She attacked me, miss. I was defending myself,' says
Sally, nursing her sore fist.

'Well, that isn't exactly what I saw,' Miss Anthony
suggests.

Almost everyone in the classroom nods.

'But miss,' continues Sally, 'she pulled me off the desk
and started attacking me. I had to punch her to get her
off.'

'Punching someone in the face is unacceptable, no matter
what the circumstances. If Renée was attacking you so
badly why didn't one of the other girls try to get her off
you? I'm going to issue you with a detention, Sally. Fighting
is unacceptable at Tudor Falls.'

'But miss, I have never had a detention. I would never start a fight,' Sally begs.

'You did start it,' I hiss. 'You and your big, nasty mouth.'

'OK, Renée, that is quite enough. You have a detention too. Both of you stay behind after school next Wednesday. I will be writing to both of your parents – guardians, that is,' she says, looking at me, 'to tell them why.' Miss Anthony walks towards the front of the class. 'Right, now, please can everyone take their seats. I have some very sad news and I need your full attention.'

Sally and I head for our desks. The temptation to pull her chair out from under her is hard to resist.

'You may have heard that Flo's father has passed away,' begins Miss Anthony.

Sally's face drops as the position of 'news breaker' is hijacked by someone with more authority.

'He was found yesterday afternoon at his home,' Miss Anthony continues.

'He was in his front garden. He was wearing his slippers,' Sally interjects, desperate to be involved in the story-telling.

'Yes, Sally. Thank you,' says Miss Anthony, silencing her. 'Flo and her family are obviously devastated at his sudden passing and so I ask you that when Flo comes back to school, when she is ready, that you all respect her and handle the situation with care. The funeral will be held on Monday, and if any of you feel that your presence will be useful and supportive for Flo, then I will happily excuse you from lessons that afternoon.'

Sally's hand shoots up. 'I will be going, Miss Anthony. I am Flo's best friend.'

'Thank you, Sally. I will make note of your absence. As Flo's best friend I hope you realise how important you are to her right now. At times like these, friends and family are everything. So take good care of your friend.' Miss Anthony nods her head as if to close that conversation. 'Right, you had all better make your way down to assembly. Renée, Sally, please come to the staffroom at lunchtime to get the confirmations of your detentions. You are all excused.'

Sally's smug look sweeps back across her face. I feel even more sorry for Flo knowing that she is stuck with that as her support system.

The rest of the day is weird. Most people are acting normally, but I can't see how they can. I keep thinking about Flo, and what she must be going through. Wondering if Julian is being nice to her, if he is OK too. Is her mum realising that she loved their dad after all? I think if Pop died Nana would die on the spot. She might be terrified of him but she can't survive without him. He keeps her alive. I don't have anyone in my life that I couldn't survive without. I have no idea if that is a good thing or a bad thing.

After school I walk home. When I arrive I go straight to the bathroom. I need the comfort of Mum's drawer. I wonder if Flo has anything similar to remind her of her dad.

When I open it I see that all of Mum's make-up has

been removed. In its place is a selection of sanitary towels and tampons.

Flo

'A neighbour found him in his front garden. Unfortunately it looks like he had a heart attack,' Miss Grut tells me gently.

'Was he wearing his slippers?' I ask, knowing that Dad would have been mortified to have been found outside with his slippers on. It really bothered him.

'I don't know, Florence. I am sure your mother will tell you everything you need to know when you get home. She says she will come and pick you up as soon as she has picked up your little sister from pre-school. You can wait in my office until she gets here. Would you like me to get you anything? A drink of water?'

I shake my head, trying to work out what she just said.

I can hear machines. The phone, the fax, the printer, they are all so loud. The windows are closed. The air is thick, I feel like I'm breathing oil. I put my hands on my face and it's wet. Where is my mother?

I breathe in more oil.

Why am I sitting in this horrible, loud, oily room? Everything suddenly becomes unbearable. Miss Grut's voice blends into all the other sounds and I have no idea what she is saying to me. I run out. I think she calls after me but I don't stop. In the school foyer I bang into a table

82

and land face down on the floor. It was hard but nothing hurts. I crawl out of the building. Then on my knees in the middle of the netball court I scream for my dad. It's cold and the sky is full of broken clouds. I scream and scream until my head hurts so much that I can't bear the sound of my own breath. There are people all around me. Someone is lifting me. I don't resist them at all.

Next thing I know I am in my kitchen. I stare at a spot on the floor. No one is saying anything. Then I hear my mother's voice.

'Well, how much is it?'

She's on the phone. Abi is playing in the living room. Julian is sitting at the other end of the kitchen table with his head in his hands.

'And when will we get it?'

She puts the phone down.

'He had life insurance. So at least that's something.'

I scan the room for objects to hit her with. I want to hammer her over the head with something, or stab her. I don't know what stops me, but I guess that's the difference between a good person and a murderer. The murderer doesn't stop themselves, but that doesn't mean that good people, like me, don't have the same thoughts sometimes.

'You have to understand the mental state he was in, Flo,' Mum says. 'He wasn't a happy man. When you do that to yourself it's basically suicide.'

The lid flies off my head.

'Do *what* to yourself? What did he *do* to himself?'

83

Mum looks at me. 'He stopped trying to please other people and then he stopped trying to please himself. Flo, this is a result of his own actions, and you will have to accept that.'

'You think he did that to *himself*?'

I feel fire come from my feet, up my legs, through my belly and into my face. It's anger so hot that it's burning holes in my clothes. I must have launched forward because now I am being pressed into the wall by Julian, and Mum is looking at me with total shock from the other side of the table. I sit, panting, as tears fall like boulders from my eyes.

How am I ever going to survive without my dad?

Renée

As I get to the end of the school lane I see Lawrence sitting on the wall waiting for me. Hasn't he got the message yet? Every step I take I dread more and more having to speak to him. Before he fell in love with me he was so funny, so in control of himself. Now he is pitiful, everything he says is delivered with puppy-dog eyes that embarrass me, and I don't want to look at him in case it encourages him, or gives him the wrong impression. Why did he have to change? And why is he still wanting to see me after I so blatantly got off with someone else in front of him? He should hate me after that.

'Hi,' he says as I get close to him.

'Lawrence, I have stuff on my mind. I think I'd like to walk home on my own.' I carry on walking past him. He doesn't take any notice of what I say and follows me.

'What's the matter?' he asks, tripping over his feet to keep up.

I want to make sure he knows that neither him nor Samuel is what is on my mind.

'Flo Parrot's dad died,' I say as I stop. 'Everyone is acting like it never happened but I keep thinking about her. I feel so sorry for her.' I stare at the ground. Too nervous to see the look on his face in case he takes it the wrong way and tells me he loves me again.

'Come here,' he says after a little bit of internal decision-making. 'Come here.'

I resist his cuddle for a few seconds but then I relax. It's nice to feel he is there for me, even if I don't really know how I feel about him. It's not like he has actually done anything wrong. I tell myself to lighten up.

'Would you like to come to my house? I'll make you cheese on toast?' he says, sounding more like the old Lawrence.

I look at him. Maybe I should give this another chance; see if he'll stop making me feel like I have to be lovey-dovey all the time. Maybe his recent behaviour is just a silly phase. With this thought I say yes, and walk with him to his house, still unsure of whether it is a good idea or not.

In Lawrence's bedroom I sit on his bed and wait for him as the smell of toast wafts in. His room is big and very tidy. Books and VHS tapes are neatly lined up along the edges on the floor, and on the far side there is a big glass tank, home to his pet snake, Frank.

I watch Frank slither around. I have always wanted a pet but I don't know why anyone would want a snake. What is the point in a pet you can't cuddle? Being alone in the room with it starts to make me feel uncomfortable. I imagine its head butting the side of the tank and shooting towards me with big sharp teeth. I feel pinned to the bed, convinced I am about to be savaged and poisoned to death. Lawrence's room is suddenly the last place I want to be.

'Here you go,' he says as he comes back in with a plate piled high with cheese on toast. 'What's the matter?'

I realise that I am pressed right up against the wall.

'Can he get out?' I say, pointing at Frank.

'Only if I take him out.'

'Why would you do that?'

'To give him a bit of freedom. I think it does him good after a big meal.'

'What does he eat?' I ask, hoping Lawrence says grass.

'Mice. I have lots of dead mice in the freezer. I drop them in and he swallows them whole. It's so cool to watch. Would you like to see?'

'NO! No, I wouldn't.' I take a piece of toast and turn myself sideways so I can't see Frank. I don't feel comfortable at all, for so many reasons. We sit and eat everything on the plate, then Lawrence gets up, puts a video in his machine, closes the curtains and says, 'Let's watch a film.'

One thing I know is that if you are in a boy's bedroom and they suggest turning the lights off and watching a film, they have no intention of watching a film at all. It's just an excuse to get you comfortable so they can try to get their hands in your pants. I immediately feel like an idiot for getting as far as his bedroom.

'Here, sit back,' he says as he plumps up his pillows and leans on them. 'Come and sit by me.'

Not feeling that I have much choice, I do what he says, and sit next to him on the bed. The film starts and I wait for a hand to start rubbing my leg. Sure enough, five minutes in and his little finger is starting to move. It's in between us, but he has slowly pressed it closer to me so it is touching my outer thigh. He is moving it up and down in a very deliberate way. After a while his whole hand joins in, and then it moves onto my thigh. It rests there for a few seconds as we both pretend this isn't happening, before creeping, very slowly, up towards my crotch. I am staring hard at the TV. I have no idea what the film is about but I am pretending to be engrossed. If I ignore him enough will he realise I don't want this and stop?

No. His fingers start to move again. Now they are right at the top of my thigh and starting to move in between them. His elbow is bent awkwardly and occasionally rubs against my boobs, and his little finger tickles me gently on my vagina. We continue to stare at the screen like it isn't happening. Am I supposed to even notice? Finally he cups me and squeezes his hand, his elbow now hitting me in the face. I am pleased as it gives me something to react to.

'Lawrence, stop it!' I say, grabbing his hand and pushing it away. I don't want to do that.'

'OK, OK, I thought you wanted to. Sorry,' he says, clearly very embarrassed. 'You give so many mixed messages to me, Renée. You met me almost every day after school for months but if I tried to do more than kiss you then you pushed me away like I was the most hideous thing ever. And you just did it again. Why did you come to my bedroom if you didn't want to do something more? It's not like you haven't done loads of stuff with other guys!'

'I haven't done *loads* of stuff with other guys!' This is only half true. I feel angry that he coaxed me here and is now turning it around, making me look bad for coming. 'Look, I don't want some drippy boyfriend who follows me around and strokes my hair, OK?

He looks visibly damaged.

'Well, I'm sorry for having feelings. It's just that you never gave the impression you didn't want me to fall in love with you, did you? You have led me on from the start, used me for fags and chips.'

'I don't *use* people for fags and chips,' I say, realising that I kind of do, and what a horrible person that makes me. I grab my blazer from the end of the bed and go to the door. I hear a loud hiss as I leave. I can't be sure if it came from Lawrence, or Frank.

4

The Importance of
Family and Friends

Flo

I know that there are lots of people sitting behind me in
the chapel but I can't face turning around. I've cried so
much and in front of so many people over the course of
the past five days that I can't bear it any more. My head
has a pain, like when you eat ice cream too quickly. My
eyes are so red I'm wondering if it might be permanent,
and I have dry skin all around my nostrils from wiping
my nose so much.

Family members have been coming to the house all
week. I've met most of them a maximum of once in my
whole life, mostly when I was a baby, so I have no memory
of them at all. They have all offered me their condolences
and told me how awful this must be for me, having been
the last person in the family to see him alive.

Is that supposed to make me feel better, or more guilty? Because in all honesty I am ridden with guilt and nothing anybody says to me is helping with that. I shouldn't have left him. I should have gone to live with him, to keep his spirits up. Abi would have been OK, she could have spent more time with us. I could have cooked for him and made him laugh, made him feel better. All he needed was some confidence, then he would have been fine. But I chose the big house over his big heart and I absolutely hate myself for it. Dad's sister Ada, who told him she would never speak to him again if he married my mother and therefore didn't, assured me there was nothing I could have done to stop his heart attack. But I think Mum is quite enjoying the idea of me thinking that there was.

The only person in our household who doesn't give me grief is Abi. She isn't at the funeral, that is one thing we all agreed on.

Dad's coffin looks too small. He was a big man, 6ft 2, wide shoulders, so why is the coffin not bigger? It is the kind of question I would have asked him had he been there. I mean there and alive, obviously.

We are gathered here today to give thanks for the life of Marcus Walter Parrot. Father to Julian, Florence and Abi, and loving husband to Theresa.

I buckle at the sound of my mum's name. I'm finding it hard to look at the vicar because he is standing so close to the coffin. I know that if I look at it the tears will come back and the thought of more crying makes my head ache even worse. I keep my head down and read the programme that Aunty Ada has put together. On the front cover, just under my dad's name and the dates 1953–1994 she has put the words:

Blessed are they that mourn: for they shall be comforted. Blessed are the meek: for they shall inherit the earth. Matthew 5:4.

Blessed are the meek? Dad was meek and he died – how is that blessed? I hear Sally cough behind me. A fake cough. A cough designed only to have people turn to look at her. Why can't she be the meek one? I bet if she died tomorrow people would say what a lovely girl she was. They'd use words like 'popular' and 'kind' and everyone in the congregation would do their best not to shout out 'SHE WAS A BITCH' because it's wrong to speak ill of the dead. But I bet that won't stop my mother speaking ill of Dad. Poor Dad. I look up. The vicar is saying a prayer. Why is that coffin so small?

Ashes to ashes. Dust to dust . . .

I recognise these words from films and TV. I know this is coming to an end. A red velvet curtain starts to spread itself around the coffin. For the first time since the service started I take in my surroundings and truly understand that my dad is inside it. As the curtain hides it I begin to panic. I didn't know that was going to happen. I didn't realise he was going to be obscured from my view like that, and taken away before I was ready. And what happens next? Where will he be burned? Does it happen right here? In this building? Will I smell it? Aunty Ada starts sobbing loudly. It's all so final. I am not prepared. I haven't said

91

goodbye; no one has said goodbye. This funeral has been too fast, so impersonal. This isn't fair on Dad.

I stand up.

'I have to say something.'

The curtain stops.

I recognise a few people from Dad's old job, and the rest are neighbours or distant family members, and others I don't know. In total I'd say there are around forty people. I want to take them all in. These are the people who have bothered to turn up to my father's funeral; in essence, these are the only people I have in the world. What a weird mix of strangers, and how lonely I feel among them. I see Sally, dressed far too revealingly for a church, looking back at me with her usual don't-make-a-fool-of-yourself-Flo face. I move my eyes away from her and try my hardest to ignore her presence. Then, right at the back, wearing her school uniform and a sort-of smile that makes the hairs on my arms stand on end, is Renée Sargent. Another fireball lights in my belly; this one feels better. I breathe in hard to put it out, focus on her eyes, and then start talking.

'I just wanted to say a few words about my dad,' I say, my tongue like sandpaper.

I get a vision of Dad in the living room, dancing to 'Chiquitita' by ABBA. Pretending to play the trombone on the umpompom bits. It used to make me laugh so much watching him, but then the vision vanishes and my eyes focus on Sally again. She is flicking her head to one side in a tiny, tense twitch, obviously suggesting I sit back down. I want to carry on but all that comes out is 'ABBA.' The rest of the words are stuck somewhere in my head. I try to reach them but they have gone. People are mumbling things. I try one more time to speak but the words are so jumbled, I can't do it. I can't say another word. I sit back down. That's it.

The curtains continue to move.

Renée

When I get home from the funeral I realise I've been so consumed in it all that I've completely missed the time. I walk in the door half an hour before school normally finishes, and am met by Pop, whose face goes from normal to bright red and veiny in under a second. As usual he presumes the worst of me before I've had a second to explain.

'Why aren't you at school, Renée?' Pop asks aggressively. 'I don't want to be back in that headmistress's office. What have you done this time? Have you been stealing again? Did you get caught smoking?'

'No, Pop. I've been to a funeral,' I say, hoping for some sympathy.

He walks closer to me. For a tiny moment I think he's going to put his arm around me and ask me if I am OK. He stops inches from my face.

'Whose funeral?'

'Flo Parrot's dad. A girl from my class. Her dad died

of a heart attack last week and I asked Miss Anthony if I could go to her funeral because I thought it was so sad,' I say, looking at him as confidently as I can manage.

'I have never heard of Flo Parrot. Who is she?' Pop scoffs.

The fact that he's never heard of her is irrelevant. I've known Carla and Gem since we were five, but almost every time Pop sees them he asks them what their names are – if he speaks to them at all. It's either a result of him not caring or his terrible memory, but Pop's memory isn't a problem. He remembers every bad thing I ever did.

'I don't want you getting involved in other people's business. Funerals are for family. It is not your place to get in the way,' Pop says dismissively.

'I wasn't in the way, Pop. I sat at the back. I just wanted to let Flo know that I cared.'

'Well, if you spent as much time caring about your grandmother and sister then that would be better. Go upstairs. Nana will call you for dinner,' he says, gently pushing me towards the stairs.

At school the next day everyone else has moved on from the death of Flo's dad. No one even mentions it. Apart from Sally, who takes great pleasure in telling everyone about the funeral – her rendition being the Hollywood movie version, of course.

'And then Flo stood up and she could hardly speak she was crying so much. And everyone was sobbing so loudly.

And Julian and I just watched her while she tried to get her words out. And then the curtain surrounded the coffin that her dad was in and it was tiny because dead people shrink. I reckon he was wearing his slippers in the coffin too.'

I can't stop thinking about Flo. I even take the long way home at night so that I can walk past her house. I don't know what I'll say if she sees me. I just feel like I know what she might be going through. I know her dad dying is completely different to my mum dying, but somewhere inside of us the feelings must be the same. Apart from Nell, I've never known anyone else who has lost a parent before. I think maybe it might be quite nice to, in a funny kind of way.

After school on Wednesday Sally and I stay behind for our detention, which she obviously blames me for entirely. I know I essentially started the fight but I was more comedy-wrestling her out of frustration. It takes a certain kind of person to actually punch someone in the face. As far as I'm concerned, this is all her fault.

'OK, girls,' starts Miss Anthony. 'I hope you have both had time to think about your behaviour last week.'

'Yes, miss,' we say together.

'And you realise that fighting, and especially punching, Sally, is unacceptable?'

'Yes, miss.'

'Good. Well, as you are both friends of Flo's and attended her dad's funeral, I thought tonight you could spend the hour writing about the importance of friends and family at times like this,' Miss Anthony says, unaware of the can of worms she just opened.

Sally looks at me like the Grand High Witch.

'Why were you there? You're not Flo's friend!'

'Now now, Sally,' warns Miss Anthony.

Sally curls her lip and shows her teeth. If Miss Anthony wasn't here I think she might have bitten me.

'Right then, girls, lets get started,' Miss Anthony continues. 'I want a whole side on the importance of friends and family in times of upset. You have an hour so I don't expect any spelling mistakes. Think carefully about what you write – I don't want to see anything crossed out. Off you go.'

I stare at the blank page. My pen seems repelled by it. What do I know about the importance of friends and family other than that family are worth avoiding in times of need, and friends don't really care that much about anything other than me being funny? It takes me about half an hour to think of something to write, by which time Sally, who has been writing furiously since Miss Anthony started the clock, slams down her pen.

The importance of friends and family in times of need
By Renée Sargent

When people feel sad, what they need is attention. Not the kind of attention where they have to be told how amazing they are all the time. Just the kind of attention where they know that should they need you,

you are there. I would like that kind of attention. I don't care about the other kind, even though everyone thinks I do.

When something horrible happens to someone the worst thing anyone can do is tell them off, or accuse them of being mean, or make them feel guilty about stuff they did that they are sorry about, because you can do bad things and be really sorry. They should just listen to them, and talk about things, because when you don't talk about things everything builds up inside you like a boiling pan with a lid on. All the water dribbles out the sides but the lid won't come off. It's like that. Life just feels like little dribbles down the side of a pan.

I think friends and families are the ones who can lift the lid off, in a good way.

I don't have time to read it over before Miss Anthony says the hour is up. I give it to her, and Sally and I leave.

'I will never forgive you for getting me a detention,' she growls as we walk out of the building.

In the car park, her dad is leaning against the bonnet of his car. His arms are crossed over his beige shirt, his moustache and beard somehow making him look even more angry. As I walk away I hear her begging him to forgive her. He doesn't sound like he is going to.

I walk home. Nana has cooked Findus Crispy Pancakes with boiled potatoes again. The pancakes are burnt around the edges. Pop eats his in under three seconds even though they are so hot steam shoots out of them when pierced with a fork. Nell eats hers slowly along with two pints of water and then excuses herself and locks herself in the bathroom. Nana says she's already eaten, and I sit there thinking, who are these people?

Flo

By Thursday Julian and I have barely said a word to each other about Dad. I decide to go to his room to chat about stuff. I need the support of my big brother. A long time ago Julian was the kind of brother who wanted to protect me, but then Mum corrupted him. She fell out of love with Dad and needed a sidekick so she took Julian and soured his brain. I guess underneath his protective personality he was less like Dad and more like her than I thought, because it didn't take long for him to become the worst ever older brother. The two of them became a force in the house, them against me and Dad. Julian and Dad fought all the time, big loud fights about respect and 'being a man'. It was all so brutish and heinous and for the last six months before Dad moved out I saw my role as protecting Abi from it all. When a row started I'd take her to her room and sing as loudly as possible. Then I'd tickle her until her own laughter blocked out the sound of the hatred downstairs.

'Can I come in?' I ask, poking my head around the door.

He's lying down playing on his Nintendo. He doesn't stop. I sit on the end of his bed to block his view of the TV.

'I miss Dad,' I say, staring right at him in a way that would be impossible to ignore.

He puts down the console and exhales like I have just asked him to loan me some money. He huffs.

'Don't you feel sad?' I ask.

Julian shrugs.

'Julian, you're just like her.' I start to cry.

He looks at me. 'Don't you have anyone else you can cry to? What about that friend of yours? The one with the white jeans? The one who carried you home that night. Go and see her.'

'Renée isn't really my friend,' I sniff.

'Well, what about the other one with the mean face and the big tits? Go cry at her.'

'Julian, our dad just died. Doesn't any part of you want to talk about it with me? You and Mum act like you wanted it to happen. Do you care at all?'

'Of course I care, Flo. But he was a mess. Maybe his heart did him a favour.'

'Julian, don't say stuff like that! He would have got himself back together eventually. He just needed to be away from Mum long enough to work out what to do. He was going to be fine.'

'Maybe he was. But I guess we will never know now, will we?'

I know. That's all that matters.

5

A Secret Affair

Flo

I go back to school exactly nine days after Dad died. No time at all really, but I feel like I've been away forever. When I walk into the classroom everyone goes quiet. Sally does an awkward skip up to me and links my arm as if to claim me before anyone else can, then leads me to my desk like she's helping a granny cross a road. Something she would never actually do.

'God, stop staring, everyone. Her dad died, she didn't grow another head.' The ease with which she says 'her dad died' shouldn't shock me as much as it does.

I sit down and she starts to arrange my things. This is very out of character, and very annoying. I sit up straight with my hands by my side and wait until she has finished.

'Best friends do this kind of thing for each other, Flo.'

'What *are* you doing?'

'What does it look like I am doing? I am organising

your things because it's all such a mess.' She empties my pencil case and puts back only half of what she has tipped out before throwing the rest in the bin. 'Less is more. When you are depressed you mustn't be surrounded by clutter.' She turns around to look at Renée, who is scratching noughts and crosses symbols onto her desk. '*This* is what friends do for each other in times of need.'

'Good morning, everybody.' Miss Anthony comes in. She looks nice. She has a tight-fitting, grey wool polo neck on with a silver brooch and a long black skirt. Seeing me at my desk, she comes over. Everyone pretends to talk while actually they are listening in.

'Welcome back, Flo. If you need anything just let me know. I'm sure Renée and Sally will take care of you until you find your feet again,' she says.

I take a sharp intake of breath. Sally's face is fluorescent red, her lip curled up to show her teeth. When that happens I know she is seriously mad. As Miss Anthony walks away Sally puts her face right up against the side of mine and says, 'If you ever become friends with Renée Sargent, I will make your life a living hell.'

Assembly is awkward. The usual shuffle is replaced by solid silence as I walk in. If I was more of an exhibitionist I might enjoy it, but the truth is I'd prefer to be invisible. I don't enjoy attention at the best of times, but a room of four hundred girls in green uniforms staring at me is oddly chilling. 'It's because they all think he killed himself' is no reassurance from Sally.

Miss Grut comes in. She is such an odd woman. I watch her, trying to work out why this stony, cold woman was the one who broke the news to me that my dad had died. It isn't that she isn't nice, she just doesn't really have a personality. I've never really seen her express anything more than slow claps and half-nods, the odd smile, and telling people off for running in the corridor. I can't imagine her being any different at home. I can't imagine her cuddling anybody, apart from her cats, which we all know she has because she is always covered in cat hair. How did my mother think it was OK that she was the one who told me my dad died?

'Sing, will you? The teachers keep looking at us,' whispers Sally and she elbows me in the ribs.

I manage to croak out a few lines of 'O Come, O Come, Emmanuel' but my tongue ties at the word 'rejoice'. I close my mouth and shut my eyes. I can feel the tears building up again. I beg myself not to cry, not here, not in assembly with Sally right next to me so desperate for me to crumble. I feel a finger tap on my left shoulder. Sally, to my right, doesn't notice. I look back. It's Renée.

'Welcome back,' she mouths. Apparently not bothered that a teacher might see.

I smile for the first time in nine days.

Renée

'Renée, can I have a word?'

When teachers pull you aside after assembly it's hardly

102

ever good news, but Miss Anthony looks surprisingly happy.

'I read your detention essay. It's really beautifully done,' she says, smiling at me.

'Thank you.' I wait for the 'But'.

'Renée,' she goes on, 'is everything OK at home? You told me a while ago that you have people to talk to, but I get the impression from your piece that might not be true. Is it true?'

'Sure, of course it is true. I mean, my grandparents aren't exactly the most expressive of people, but we get on OK. And I have friends. Loads of friends. I was just practising my creative writing a bit. In real life I've got loads of friends,' I say quickly.

If ever there was an 'I don't believe you' face, then Miss Anthony is pulling it.

'OK, Renée. Well, I'm always here should you need to talk. And if that is a bit much for you then I think you could use writing a bit more, to get things off your chest.' She stops. There's a little furrow on her brow. 'When my mother died I was so angry but I couldn't talk about it, so I wrote it all down. I wrote letters to all the people that I felt had let me down. I never intended to give the letters to them, but getting everything on to paper really helped me make sense of it all. You write really nicely about your feelings. Maybe you could try it?'

It is really nice to be told I am good at something. Even if it isn't something I can get a GCSE for.

'Thanks, Miss Anthony. I'll give it ago. Can I ask you something?'

'Of course.'

'Do you still miss your mum?'

'I'm not sure I miss her, but I think about her every day,' Miss Anthony says slowly. 'It's just a part of who I am. Does that makes any sense?'

I nod. That makes sense to me. That is how I am starting to feel. I miss missing her a bit at the moment though. It makes me feel bad.

The bell rings.

'Thanks, Miss Anthony.' I walk away.

'Oh, and Renée,' Miss Anthony calls back. 'I imagine you make a fine friend to other people too. Flo is lucky to have you.'

'I'm lucky to have Flo,' I say, feeling like a total fraud.

I take my place on the front bench of the science lab. A few weeks ago we had been dissecting pigs' trotters and all the vegetarians were huddled in a corner trying not to look. I thought it would be funny to flick a bit of trotter at them from the end of my ruler. As it turned out, it wasn't very funny. I only meant it as a joke but it landed inside Kerry Bowden's pencil case and she screamed like someone had run over her foot.

Vegetarians are so dramatic. What's it all about anyway? I mean, I respect animals, but I also respect the food chain, and one of the few pleasures I have living with Nana and Pop is that once a week I'm allowed to have a tin of Chicken in White Wine Sauce with a pouch of Uncle Ben's rice. I have the whole tin, in a bowl, poured on top of the rice and I sprinkle so much salt on it that not all of it dissolves. The reason I love the Chicken in White Wine Sauce so much is because Nana gives it to me while Pop is at the snooker hall on Thursdays, and she lets me eat it with a spoon sitting on the floor next to the heating vent, because that is my favourite place. That fifteen minutes once a week is my idea of heaven. Not only does tinned Chicken in White Wine Sauce taste like the most delicious thing ever – with the possible exception of Wotsits – but Nana only has to heat it up, so even she can't ruin it.

Nell has recently announced that she is a vegetarian. When she told Pop he shouted at me for filling her head with nonsense, and Nana cried. I think everyone in my family is actually starting to lose their minds.

When Mrs Suiter turns to write something on the blackboard, something light hits me on the back.

Hey!
Thanks for coming to Dad's funeral. I don't know why you came but I am really glad you did. I'm sorry if I was weird with you in the field that time. I guess I am quite jealous of you really. Anyway, I just wanted to say thanks for coming. It was really nice that you did x

My belly does a little flip and I get goosebumps on my arms. I'm so used to people translating every nice thing I ever do as me trying to get something for myself that I just presume people think the worst of me all the time. I have been wanting to apologise to Flo for ages about how mean I was to her that day we ate chips together. I think I just got defensive because she was right – I don't really do anything apart from mess about.

That's OK! I'm sorry I took the piss out of you for playing the clarinet. I actually think it's quite cool that you play an instrument x

I wait for Mrs Suiter to turn around and throw it at Flo. Seconds later it's back.

Chips after school?

I turn around to smile and nod.

Flo

I see Renée waiting for me at the end of the school lane. I observe her more in these few seconds than I ever have before. Renée is really pretty but a bit of a mess. Her skirt is above the regulation length, and both of her brown knee-length socks are scrunched down at her ankles. Her white shirt is untucked and hanging below her jumper, and her tie is loose. She's wearing a blazer despite the cold – almost everyone else comes to school in their duffel coats at this time of year. Above her round face her hair is messy and brown with a fringe that's too long. Her eyes are dark and her smile is wide and cheeky, with dimples on both of her cheeks. She leans against the wall with one foot pressed against it, her bag on the ground even though it's muddy, smoking a cigarette.

We first make eye contact when I'm halfway down the lane. She doesn't take her eyes off me, and I walk towards her awkwardly.

'Hey.'

'Hey.'

She picks up her bag. Not even checking to see if it's got muddy, which it has.

'So, what do you want to do?' she says as she swings it over her shoulder and sprays mud on her socks.

'Honestly, whatever you want. I don't mind.' I hate myself for being so indecisive.

'OK, let's go to the beach. Do you want a fag?'

I shake my head. 'No thanks. I don't smoke.'

'I like the smell of smoke,' she says, blowing a perfect smoke ring. 'On the right person it smells lovely.'

We walk down the huge hill into St Peter Port, passing the boys' school on the way. They're all coming out, looking so smart in their grey suits. Julian used to go there, but he left after his GCSEs to work as a mechanic. I can't imagine any of this lot fixing cars, they all look like lawyers or bankers. No wonder Julian never fitted in, these aren't his kind of people at all.

We don't say much while we walk through the sea of boys. Renée links her arm into mine and leads me through them like she has done this a thousand times. Then one calls after us. He looks angry.

'Renée?'

'Keep walking,' she says. 'I don't want to talk to him.'

'Who is he?'

'It doesn't matter. Just keep walking.'

'Renée, WAIT. Renée.' He is pretty determined to get her attention but not as determined as she is to get away from him. As his voice gets louder she makes more of an effort to avoid him. Then she slips her arm out, grabs my hand and screams.

'RUUUUNNNNN!'

We run down past the Sunken Gardens, past the courtrooms, down onto Smiths Street and past the post office, then we take a sharp right and run all along the cobbled high street. She is pulling me along so fast my feet leave the ground a few times and it's a miracle I don't fall flat on my face. Eventually she pulls me into a tiny alleyway with steep steps that lead to the waterfront. Bent double and panting, I manage to catch my breath.

'What was that about? Who was that boy?' I ask, intrigued.

She can barely speak.

'Lawrence.' Her breathing starts to stabilise. 'Do you think he got the message?'

'Did he get the message? I think the whole school got it. I take it he wasn't very nice to you then?'

'He told me he loved me,' she says, still out of breath.

'Isn't that good?' I ask, confused.

'It's only good if you feel it back. If you don't feel it back it's just annoying. Come on, let's get chips.'

I follow her, feeling a bit unsure of what Lawrence did that was so wrong. I think I'd quite like someone to tell me they loved me.

Renée

With our chips, we walk along the seafront and end up at Havelet Bay, a beach just south of town and at the bottom of a huge hill with lots of bends that Mum and Nell and I used to call the Wiggly Woggly Road. When Mum drove up or down it Nell and I stood behind each of the seats, holding onto the head rests, leaning to one side shouting 'Wiiiiigggggglllllyyyyyy', then when we went round the next bend we would swing to the other side and shout 'Woooogggggglllly'. The idea was that we couldn't move or start the next word until the car had started to turn. After Mum died I'd do this in the car with Pop, but he'd shout at me to sit down and shut up. So that was the end of that.

'Let's sit on the wall and dangle our feet over the edge,' I say, climbing up onto the high sea wall.

'But it's so high!' says Flo, looking up at me.

'I know it's high, but what is the worst that can happen?'

'Um, I fall off and drown?'

Fair point. But I still don't get down.

Havelet wall is high, but so is the tide, so the fall isn't

that big. And anyway, people jump off it all the time. It's a 'thing'. There are no rocks, so unless you bang your head on the way down or forget how to swim you can't really go wrong. Not that I've ever done it. Pop caught me down here last year with a bunch of surfer boys and dragged me away making me promise I would never, ever jump. So I haven't. But I don't know why I keep my promises to Pop. He promised Mum on her deathbed that he would take care of me, and even though I live in his house and he pays for my food, I don't think ignoring my feelings and making me feel like a continuous pain in his arse is taking care of me. So maybe I shouldn't care so much about the promises I make to him.

'Let's jump,' I say, looking at Flo.

'Don't be crazy,' she replies adamantly.

'Why not? People do it all the time. I know the water will be cold, but I've never seen anyone get out saying it isn't amazing. Let's do it.'

'But what about our uniforms?' says Flo, looking anxious. 'We can't walk home drenched. And there is no way I am stripping off. And it's freezing!'

I start to take my clothes off.

'We can leave our jumpers, skirts and coats up here. Our shoes will stop the other stuff blowing away. We can jump in, swim to the beach, run back up here and put our coats on to wear home. Come on, Flo.'

'I can't, Renée. I don't do this kind of thing. You jump, I'll hold your clothes. NO, don't jump. This is crazy. It isn't safe.'

'I'm sick of being safe. I'm bored all the time. Come on, Flo. Haven't the last few weeks taught you anything? We have to live our lives. Keep pushing ourselves, take risks, be silly. If Madonna was here, she'd jump.'

'What's Madonna get to do with anything?'

'Flo, are you coming or not?' I stand up straight on the wall, my legs slightly apart. I'm eye level with the sky. It's peaceful up here. I close my eyes. I'm going to take three deep breaths and jump. I can do this. Sod Pop and his rules. This is my life and I will live it my way. ONE . . . TWO . . .

'Wait. Wait for me.'

Flo tears off her coat, jumper and shoes. After folding them up neatly (mine are in a heap) she takes my hand. I pull her up and we stand next to each other on the wall. After a few deep breaths I turn to her. She's pure white and clearly terrified.

'Are you ready?'

'I'm ready. No, wait. Oh my God. OK, I am ready.'

'ONE, TWO, THREEEEEEEE.'

Hand in hand, we jump off the wall and into the sea.

Flo

When I walk into school, Sally does her usual act of speaking to me like the sole purpose of my existence on earth is to be her sidekick.

'Have you been practising the second part for our

111

clarinet lesson? My solo is perfect now.' She says it like that makes her the Queen or something.

'Actually, I'm not sure I want to play the clarinet any more. I'm never going to be in an orchestra, so what's the point?' I tell her firmly.

'You WHAT?' Sally's face seems to get bigger, and she shows her teeth. If this was a cartoon steam would shoot out of her ears.

'Yeah, the clarinet just isn't for me. I'm not going to come to the lessons any more. Sorry,' I say. I can't quite believe how much I'm enjoying making her squirm.

She is literally dumbstruck. This is me making a decision for myself, and she has no idea how to deal with it.

She grumbles and mumbles like a mad old lady all the way down to assembly. I just keep focusing on yesterday when I jumped off the wall with Renée. Up on that wall, nothing mattered.

When Miss Grut comes in she has her serious face on. I mean, her face is always serious, but this face looks more serious than usual. Everyone stands and waits to hear whatever it is she is obviously upset about.

'Ladies, your full attention, please. The bad behaviour of two students has been brought to my attention. Yesterday just after school, two Tudor Falls pupils were seen jumping off the wall at Havelet Bay. The two girls were not identified, but their uniforms were recognised to be ours and I am now suggesting that the two girls responsible come to my office immediately after assembly and own up to this very irresponsible and dangerous behaviour. Should the perpetrators of this activity be you, or someone you know, then let me tell you that not coming forward will have you in much deeper trouble in the long run than admitting to it now. Has anyone got anything they would like to tell me?'

There is a long pause.

'No? Right, well, I trust that those who are responsible will realise how serious this is and come to my office. OK, ladies, the Lord's Prayer, please. *Our Father . . .*'

'Whoever did that is in soooooo much shit,' whispers Sally.

I feel sick. I have never done anything so bad and I'm terrified of the trouble I'm going to get into over it. This is the kind of thing people get expelled for. I don't want to get expelled. I want to pass all my GCSEs so that I can go to university. I've ruined everything. I feel like a criminal about to get convicted for doing the most awful thing imaginable. I will be expelled and I'll have to go and work in a shop. And Sally will come in and spend all her dad's money and laugh at me for being such a loser with no GCSEs, and I'll have to stay in Guernsey forever. Living with Mum because I don't have the money to move out. And, and . . .

Oh my God, why did I jump? Why, WHY DID I JUMP? What a mess. I look down the row from left to right, searching for Renée, then I look behind me to my right. I feel so conspicuous. Every move I make seems guilty, and I am guilty, SO guilty. I look back and then to my left. There is Renée, already meeting my eyes. She doesn't appear remotely worried. In fact, she looks happy. She winks at me. Winks?

113

I turn back to the front. My breath is becoming harder to keep quiet, then I hear a voice, my dad's voice. He says, *Remember how good it felt to jump?* And then I realise, I realise that even getting expelled can't make me regret the fact that I jumped off the wall. Jumping off the wall was the best thing I ever did and no amount of trouble is going to make me regret it. I turn to Renée and wink back. Maybe I *am* the kind of person who jumps off walls.

At break time I find a note in my bag.

Wanna hang out after your clarinet lesson?

I'm so excited I do an involuntary star jump.

Renée

As Flo walks towards me I feel really self-conscious of how I'm standing. Am I slouching? Nana always tells me I slouch. I push my shoulders back against the wall and press one foot into it. I don't know what to do with my hands so I light a fag. Should I watch her walk towards me, or should I turn away and then look up at the last minute and act surprised? I decide to watch her the whole way. She walks as quickly as she can. This is good as it cuts down the length of awkward eye contact, but it does mean she looks kind of silly.

It's raining, so neither of us wants to go to the beach. Instead we head to the Sunken Gardens, just at the bottom of the Grange before town. It means we have to get past the boys' school again.

'You won't make me run again, will you? I'll definitely fall over in this rain. For someone who skives cross-country you sure seem to love running,' says Flo.

'Cross-country is different, you're not trying to get anywhere. It's pointless running.'

I link my arm through hers and we set off, sharing her brolly. As we get near the boys' school they're all piling out as usual. Even though I really don't want to see Lawrence I hope that some of the boys notice me. Seeing as Lawrence is nowhere to be seen, I make sure Flo and I walk nice and slowly.

'Let's enjoy this. We're the only girls around,' I tell her.

I hold the umbrella up high so they can see our faces. Then, pretending not to be bothered by their attention, I wiggle my bottom ever so slightly and hold eye contact with anyone who looks my way. Flo, on the other hand, is rigid. When I look at her face she looks like she's about to be run over.

'What's the matter?' I say.

'What? Nothing? I'm cool.'

It occurs to me, Flo has no idea how to flirt.

'Relax,' I tell her. She goes completely floppy and does the fakest smile I've ever seen. 'No, just relax. Just be the Flo who jumped off the wall.'

This seems to have an effect on her. She straightens her back and holds up her head. She's more like a regimental soldier than a confident young woman, but it's better than the made-of-jelly routine she was just doing. We walk slowly through the crowd of boys, and giggle at the whistles.

'See? Nice to be noticed, isn't it?' I say, giving her a gentle nudge.

'They're looking at you, not me. I'm as sexy as a plank of wood.'

That isn't true. Flo *is* sexy, she just hasn't been allowed to notice that about herself yet. She's skinny but her boobs are big. Her hair is lovely and long, and a deep chestnut brown. Her eyes are smallish but when she puts the right thought behind them they really light up. And sure, her nose is a bit big but her lips are too, and boys love big lips. She seems almost embarrassed by them though.

'My lips take over my face. Well, the bits of my face that my nose doesn't take over, anyway,' she says, like she really dislikes herself.

'You need to realise how gorgeous you are.'

She laughs, but I'm not trying to be funny. 'I mean it, Flo, you really are. Somewhere under all that disbelief.'

'No one has ever said *that* to me before. Sally went through a stage of calling me Humpty Dumpty.'

'Well, Sally is an arsehole,' I say, wishing that Sally's name never had to come up.

'Dad used to tell me I was beautiful,' Flo says as she stops walking and drops her head. I feel guilty for making her think about her dad. I move her by her shoulders so we're facing each other.

'Well, I think your dad was right.'

116

I hug her, the umbrella on the ground next to us. There's a chorus of 'Look at the lezzers' coming from the boys, who are still just feet away, but neither of us seems to care. We stand there, hugging in the rain.

Flo

By the time we get to the Sunken Gardens we are soaking wet. Hiding from the rain in one of the shelters, we start to read the graffiti.

Renée and Lawrence Woz 'Ere.

'You must have liked him at one point then? Writing your names on the wall is pretty permanent,' I say, still unsure of what Lawrence did that was so wrong.

'Yeah, we used to have loads of fun. Until he got all serious.'

'Why is someone telling you they loved you so awful?' I ask.

'It's not just that he told me he loved me, it's more about how he expected me to say it back. I don't like feeling cornered into saying stuff I don't feel and doing stuff I don't want to do. And anyway, love at our age is ridiculous,' Renée says, tapping her toe in a puddle of water.

Putting it like that it makes more sense. People live whole lives together pretending to be in love. I guess Mum

117

and Dad did that for most of their relationship. Then they realised they couldn't pretend any more but they were stuck with each other, and look where that got them. I've never really thought about love being such a big deal before. I just presumed that if someone was kind enough to say it to me, I would be kind enough to say it back, but maybe you shouldn't just say 'I love you'. You have to mean it.

'Shall we write something?' says Renée, waving a marker pen at me.

I surprise myself by taking the pen. Graffiti? What's happened to me?

'What will we write? I'm not writing the word "woz",' I say, making sure she knows I do have limits.

'OK, no "woz".'

She takes a moment to think, tapping the end of the pen on her bottom lip. Her lips are really dark pink, like she has lipstick on, but she doesn't. Her brain is ticking over, her eyes look mischievous, then serious, then confused. Then she puts the pen to the wall and starts writing.

Renée ♥ Flo

She does a big full stop after it, puts the lid back on the marker and says, 'There!' She looks very proud of herself. I don't know what I am supposed to say. We sit down.

'Is that weird?' she asks, after a few minutes.

'What?'

118

'That I drew a heart. Especially after my speech about love being ridiculous at our age. I didn't know what else to put. It's OK when it's for friends, isn't it? It's not like I'm sitting here desperate for you to tell me you love me or anything.' She does an awkward laugh.

My tummy is flipping at the thought of Sally seeing it. She would kill me. Do I care? Annoyingly I do. She loves having an excuse to make me feel even more crap about myself than I do already. It's validation for her, and torture for me. Being friends with Renée Sargent will give her the ultimate ammunition.

'No, it's fine. It's nice,' I say, not wanting to make Renée feel bad. 'What shall we talk about?'

The rain is getting heavier. We are sheltered from it but I wonder if I have a plastic bag in my school bag that I can use to cover my hair for the walk home. I start to look, but drop my bag when she casually says, 'SEX?'

My throat tightens. I bet Renée has got off with loads of boys. What am I supposed to talk about in a conversation about sex? I don't think I've ever had a conversation about sex.

'Have you ever done it?' I ask, trying to make it as much about her as possible.

'No. Not full sex, but I have done everything else.'

'Like what? Have you done blow jobs?' I ask, feeling silly for saying blow jobs out loud.

'Yeah, they're all right. You just have to shut your eyes and hold your breath. It never takes long.'

'How do you know when to stop?'

'Oh wow, you really haven't done anything, have you?' she says, trying to stop herself laughing at me.

The truth is I haven't. Sally has never let me get close enough to anyone to even try. And she makes me feel so stupid and insecure, and fat and ugly, that unless I'm out of my brain like I was under that bush with Samuel, then I just don't have the confidence to get to do that stuff with a boy. I avoid her question.

'Why didn't you do it with Lawrence?' I ask.

'Because I didn't want to. He would be my first and I don't want to regret it. But who knows if it will work out that way. I guess it will depend on how drunk I am when the moment comes.'

She laughs, but she isn't really joking.

'Renée, you will tell me when you have sex for the first time, won't you? I think we both know you will do it first.'

'Sure, friends tell each other everything, right?'

'Right!'

She draws a noughts and crosses grid on the wall and we start to play. I win.

Renée

'Margaret,' I whisper loudly as I poke my head out of the cloakroom. 'The dark ones, just the dark ones.'

She crawls along the corridor on her hands and knees, digging out the carpet tiles with a biro and holding them under her arm as she goes.

120

'How many have you pulled up?' she shouts back, thinking that she whispered it. I turn to Flo, who has six tiles in her hand, and relay it back to Margaret.

It's lunchtime, and while everyone else is downstairs in the dining room, we are upstairs swapping the carpet tiles in the corridor with the different-coloured ones in the cloakroom. Why this amuses us so much I am not quite sure, but Margaret and I have done it for years. We are the Phantom Carpet Shifters, and for years teachers have tried to catch us in the act. People speculate that it's us, and Miss Trunks has even checked my fingernails for bits of fluff before, but until they catch us, we are innocent. This time is the most fun ever though, because Flo is with us too.

'I can't believe it was you all this time,' she says. 'I used to think this was so funny, but Sally said whoever did it was immature.'

We lay the dark red tiles in the spots where the beige ones used to be and press them down with our feet.

'Why is this so fun?' asks Flo. We laugh, unable to answer the question. It just is.

'Teeeeeaaaaacccchhhheeerrrrrr!' screeches Margaret as she runs back in and dives under all the duffel coats that have fallen off their pegs. Like clockwork I get under the pile on the other side of the room, completely forgetting that Flo doesn't have my ingrained hiding tactics. From my spot on the floor, I watch her through a buttonhole as she runs awkwardly around the cloakroom with one last tile in her hands.

121

'Flo Parrot! Of all the girls to find I never expected it to be you,' says Miss Le Hurray as she storms in. Flo drops what she is holding like it is made of fire. She looks terrified. I feel so bad that she is left to take the blame. Just as I'm about to creep out from under the pile of coats and fess up to years of carpet tile rearranging, Flo starts to speak.

'Yes. It was me. It was me swapping the carpet tiles all along.'

What is she doing?

'It's always been me. Just me. I've done it for years,' Flo says proudly.

For a moment Miss Le Hurray looks at her like she might be joking. But a confession is a confession, and there isn't much to question when Flo gets down on her hands and knees and starts pressing in the last red tile from the corridor floor into a gap.

'Right, I see. Please stop that now, Flo, and follow me downstairs. I am taking you to see Miss Grut.'

Flo follows her out of the cloakroom, turning back at the last second to wink at the pile of coats that she knows I am underneath. I wait to hear the double doors shut before I move.

'PHEW, that was a close one,' says Margaret in a voice that makes me wonder if she had been holding her breath the entire time.

'Yeah, phew,' I reply, emotional and amazed that Flo took the blame for us. I hurry downstairs and sit opposite Miss Grut's office, pretending to read a magazine about careers. Eventually Flo comes out.

'What happened?' I ask.

'Nothing,' Flo tells me nonchalantly. 'She just thinks I am acting up because of what happened to Dad. I got a warning and had to promise not to move any more carpet tiles. Maybe you and Margaret should stop doing it now. I think I would get into a lot of trouble if it happened again.'

'No, sure. Of course. Thank you!' I still can't quite believe Flo did that.

'It's fine.' Flo grins. 'It's hardly the crime of the century, is it? It was quite exciting. I have to go and put them all back now. You could help me with that?'

We head back upstairs, and when all of the tiles are back where they should be, I nip to the loo, leaving Flo sitting on a pile of duffel coats eating an apple. I can't stop smiling.

As I am coming back into the cloakroom I stop when I hear voices.

'What do you mean you had lunch up here? Why?' It's Sally's voice. She sounds annoyed, as usual.

'I just wanted some peace and quiet, that's all,' Flo tells her.

'I think what happened to your dad has made you go a bit funny lately. Anyway, come on. I want to go through our history prep for this afternoon.'

I hear them both leave the cloakroom with absolutely no resistance from Flo. It wipes the smile right off my face.

6

Men Come and Go

Renée

I am loaded up with crisps. I have three packets of Quavers, two of Wotsits, one cheese and onion Walkers and one salt and vinegar Walkers. After five weeks of secretly meeting Flo almost every day after school, I now know that she eats all of the Wotsits. So I always buy two packets. We start with a packet of those each, then tear open all the other packets and share them while we talk about life in general. She usually eats most of the cheese and onion ones and today is no different. I don't mind, I like salt and vinegar the most. We are sitting on the back of someone's boat in the marina facing the town. A white stripy canopy is sheltering us from the rain and the other boats act as windbreaks, making this boat an unlikely hideout from the cold.

'What's the most embarrassing thing about your body?' I ask, my mouth full of crisps.

124

She stops chewing and looks at me suspiciously.

'Come on. I'll tell you mine if you tell me yours,' I press.

She takes a deep breath, exhales just as fast and with a surprising level of calm says, 'I have a long dark hair growing out of my right nipple.'

I spit a mouthful of Quavers out into the sea. They congeal on the surface and get further mashed by the rain that's falling out of the sky like dead birds. A rogue Quaver wedges itself in my throat, making me hack as I bend forward trying to cough it up. Flo doesn't help me by slapping me on the back. When I catch my breath, red faced and still horrified, I manage to eek out, 'SERIOUSLY?'

'Well, you asked,' Flo says, sounding a bit cross.

'Wait, but what do you mean? Like a head hair or a pube? And out of what part of your nipple?'

'I guess it's a bit pubey. It's thicker than the ones on my head and it goes out of the bit around my nipple. Renée, STOP laughing at me. You asked me, I was honest, and now you will tell everyone and I'll never live it down!'

She slumps back. For a moment I presume she is joking, but then she starts to cry. Really cry. Like the rain.

'That's just what I need, another friend who thinks I am hideous,' she says through her tears.

I feel awful.

'I don't think you're hideous, Flo. I was just shocked that you went straight in there with the nipple hair thing. I wasn't expecting it, that's all.'

'But you asked me what the most embarrassing thing

125

on my body is. I was being honest. Now I feel like a giant freak.'

I snuggle up as close to her as I can. 'I love you for your honesty,' I tell her.

She sniffs and wipes her eyes.

'Anyway, I'm not one to judge, I have to bleach my big toes with Nana's moustache cream because they're so hairy. Oh, and look.' I lean over to rest on one buttock and pull down the side of my school skirt, simultaneously lifting up my shirt. 'Look, I have terrible stretch marks. I hate them so much I never want to be naked, ever.' My stretch marks are purple and shimmery and I'm sure they're getting worse. I have them on my sides, inside my thighs and on my boobs. 'I think *I* am the gross one. At least you can pluck your hair out. I'm stuck with these forever.'

She stares at them, really stares. Showing my stretch marks to someone is my biggest fear, but I owed it to her after laughing so hard at her nipple. She unfolds her arms, obviously reassured that me baring my stretch marks means I'm not going to tell everyone about her right boob.

'You can put them away now.' She pauses. 'You're just a bit stripy, right? Stripes are pretty. If they really bother you I won't pluck my nipple hair out so we are equal. How's that?'

'Deal,' I say, and we eat some more crisps. 'Thanks for being sweet about my stretch marks. I feel way better about them now.' I pause for a few long seconds. 'But pluck that hair out of your nipple. Please?'

She thumps me on my arm.

As we walk towards home her brolly is torn inside out by a massive gust of wind. This winter on Guernsey is particularly brutal. Pop says it is the sea air reminding us that we are nothing in the grand scheme of things, and that we are at the mercy of nature at all times. Trust him to remind me that there's no point in bothering with life at all.

We walk into the rain, our arms linked and our heads pushing through it like snow ploughs. It's too cold to have a conversation so we focus on the top of the hill where we say goodbye most days when we split to go our separate ways. Just as we are reaching it, Flo screams and drags me off the pavement and behind a bush. With twigs tangled in my hair and leaves in my mouth I spit and splutter until I manage to ask her what on earth she thinks she is doing.

'That was Sally's mum's car. It was coming right towards us. Thank God we were near this bush. I should have known she would come this way after clarinet. Phew!' She is pleased with herself.

With half a tree stuck in my hair I'm struggling to see the brilliance of our situation.

'Great. Well, I'm glad she didn't see us. God forbid you will ever be honest about us,' I huff.

I storm back into the rain. I'm so angry I could scream at full volume in her face. What is Flo's problem!?

'Renée, wait. What's wrong?'

'What's wrong? Are you mental? We have met almost

127

every day after school for over a month. We tell each other everything. You take the rap for bad things I do, we have this amazing time together and then all day in classes you ignore me like I don't exist. And I have to watch you and Sally together, and you licking her arse and not telling her about me. And when she says something mean to me you just stand there. I don't even answer back like I used to, I take it and you just stand there and let her speak to me the way she does. What about the fact that I am your best friend now? How do you think that feels, Flo? It feels HORRIBLE, that is how it feels. HORRIBLE.'

I leave her standing in the rain. I deliberately go slowly so she can catch me up, but she doesn't. I get all the way home and she never comes after me. The smell of burnt pastry wafts into my face as I open the door of the house.

We eat our dinner to the sound of Pop grunting like a pig. Nell looks agonised by her own thoughts, her cheekbones like fists under her skin. Nana seems to have no concept of how bad the dinner she has cooked us tastes. Then Nell starts talking.

'I'm thinking about getting in touch with Dad. I want to see him.'

Pop slams down his cutlery. Nana stiffens like a corpse. I close my eyes.

'I have the right to see my own father. It isn't his fault he left. You made him,' Nell continues.

She is in one of her provocative moods. Statements like

this can only go one way in our house. She wants to cause a fight, a big fight. She's decided tonight is the night.

'I want his phone number. I know you have it. I want to see him and you have to let me.'

Pop's lid flies off, I swear I see it. He stands up and crashes his hands down on the table. He pushes his face forward and right up close to Nell's. I remain silent.

'Your father made his own choice. He ran off with some Spanish tart and left us to deal with his mess.'

'Is that what we are? His mess? Mum's mess?' says Nell, getting louder and more determined. She screams. A long, loud, frustrated scream that makes me cover my ears with my hands. Then she runs upstairs and locks herself in the bathroom.

Pop sighs very loudly, then turns to me. 'What nonsense have you been filling her head with for her to say those things?'

'I haven't said anything to her, Pop. That's how she feels.'

'Go and do some revision or you'll fail everything. Then what will people say about me? That I didn't bring you up right?' he says as he points at the door.

'That's right, love. Go and do your schoolwork. The exams aren't far away now,' Nana says quietly.

I sit on my bed listening to Nell sobbing in the bathroom and Pop's voice bellowing and plates smashing, as he deals with his anger the only way he knows how.

Flo

I didn't run after Renée because I couldn't tell her what she wants to hear. When I thought Sally was going to see me with her I panicked. I felt like the ground was opening up and I was going to get sucked in.

Renée thinks it will be easy to tell Sally, but if I do then I will still have to sit next to her for the rest of the year. We will still be in the same classes for everything but science and she will never let us just get on with being friends. The only way Renée and I can keep seeing each other is to keep it secret. Maybe over time I can phase out my friendship with Sally, maybe by the time we come back for sixth form she will have found someone else to boss around, and Renée and I can sit next to each other and then it will all be fine, but it's how we get to that which terrifies me. I need her to give me more time. Sally is not someone you just break news to. There's a system. I just need to work out what that system is.

When I get back to the house I'm soaking wet and starving. Mum has recently decided that ready meals are the best way to feed me, so the fridge is full of them. I hate ready meals. Dad used to cook big dinners before he moved out, but Mum never ate much of them. She lived on a diet of coffee and fags. Spaghetti bolognese, chicken curry, lasagne – if I concentrate hard enough I can still smell them. I inhale deeply and imagine the smell filling the house. Following my nose into the kitchen I dream of the meals Dad used to cook, but I don't quite make it to the fridge.

'Flo,' says Mum in a stern voice. She is sitting at the head of the kitchen table. There is a man leaning against the sink. I don't recognise him. 'This is Fred. He is going to come and live with us. OK?'

I fall silent for what feels like half an hour. Neither of them offer to chat through it. Move in? Already? The house still smells of Dad.

'What do you mean, live with us? In Dad's house?'

'It isn't your dad's house any more. It's my house, and yes, Fred is going to come and live with us in this house.'

I hear a banging in the hallway. Two men carry Mum's mattress down the stairs, and a new one is shortly brought back in. I watch this while we stand in another cold pool of silence.

'Hello, Flo. Nice to meet you.' Fred reaches out a hand to me. I shake it. His palms are clammy and his eyes are creepy. He is tall and his face is shiny. His hair isn't blond but it isn't brown, it's browny-grey. A bit of it is combed over his head to hide some baldness, but it's thin and pointless really, I can see his skin through it. I don't say anything at all.

'We are going to go to France for a few days,' says Mum. 'We leave tonight. The childminder will have Abi while you're at school but you need to take over when you get home tomorrow. I'll be back lunchtime Thursday. OK?' Mum's tone suggests I have no choice but to agree.

131

'OK,' I say like a robot. I'm stunned and unable to do much more than stand there looking at them.

They both leave the kitchen and go upstairs. My appetite has gone.

I go into the living room. Julian is watching TV and drinking a beer.

'Julian, do you know about this man who is going to live with us?' I still have something of the robot about me.

'Fred. Yes. Mum met him at work. He's all right.'

'She is supposed to go to work to get money to feed us all. Not to get a man to live with us all. What is happening?' I'm shocked by how unconcerned he is by Fred.

'She doesn't have to work any more. The life insurance came through. Everything's fine now,' Julian tells me.

'*Everything is fine now?* Excuse me? Is Dad being dead, Mum being rich off the back of it and some random bald man with more hair coming out the end of his nose than on his head suddenly living with us the definition of *fine*?'

He doesn't offer the slightest hint that he cares.

'And when are we going to spread Dad's ashes? I can't keep looking at them in that box on the mantelpiece. Shall we spread them down at the harbour? I think he would like to be in the sea.'

'You can if you want.'

He doesn't look up. I pick up the box.

Our dead dad is in this box. Our dead dad. In this box. Burnt into little pieces of ash. His face, his hands, his legs, his feet, all of them, they are all in this box. It's so weird.

Weeks ago he was a human being and now he is just a pile of ash in a little brown wooden box.

'Julian?' I say.

'WHAT, Flo?'

For once he looks at me. A mean, hard stare that makes me feel as uncomfortable as he intended me to feel. If I was holding anything else in the entire world I'd throw it at him, but Dad deserves better than to be anywhere near him. I leave the room and take the box with me. I don't want Dad to be around Julian or Mum, or that guy called Fred who now lives in my house who I hate.

The next morning at school I can tell that Renée is angry. Usually she does something to get Sally out of the way so she can pass me a note, like put her pencil case on the other side of the room when she goes to the loo, but today she does nothing. I love her notes, I'll keep them forever. Renée says she does the same, and that one day when we are older and live somewhere cool like London, we'll read them all out to each other and laugh about how young and silly we were.

She is being quiet. No notes, no cheeky grin. She keeps her head down during registration and she doesn't sing the hymn really loudly in assembly to make everyone laugh like she usually does. I know I've upset her and it's horrible. My life has changed so much over the last month. I lost the most important person in my entire world and when I thought that I would never survive it Renée was just there, distracting me from all of it. I don't know what would have happened to me if the only person I had to talk to was Sally. My heart might have stopped, like Dad's.

As we sit waiting for Miss Anthony to arrive, Sally won't stop talking. 'Dad has a new colleague. His name's Phil, he's twenty-seven. I can tell he fancies me. Last night he came round for dinner, and when I went to bed he told my dad to make sure I gave him a kiss goodnight when I had my nightie on.'

'What did your dad say?' I ask, thinking that the guy sounds a bit creepy.

'He laughed. It was funny, but I know Phil wasn't joking. I really think he fancies me.'

The sound of her voice is having the same effect on me as Chinese water torture. I really need her to stop talking or go away. 'You have something in your teeth,' I say, to which she is up and out of the classroom so quick that even I am shocked by her vanity. Apparently having something in your teeth is the worst thing imaginable. When she's out of the way I scribble a note, fold it up, and lob it at Renée.

I'm sorry. You are my best friend. Come to my house after school. Please x

She picks it up slowly and reluctantly unfolds it. After staring at it for ages she refolds it and throws it into her desk. No cheeky looks, no smile. Does she hate me?

'There is nothing there. Idiot.' Sally is back.

134

'There was. A poppy seed or something. Or maybe it was just dirt.'

'I do not have dirt in my mouth!'

She spins around and stomps her way up to our maths lesson. I take three deep long breaths and prepare myself to follow her. Just as I'm about to go a note hits me on the back of the head.

See you at the end of the lane x

Renée

I couldn't stay mad at Flo for long. Who am I to pretend that telling people how you feel is easy? I think Pop is hard to talk to, but Sally is a whole new level of crazy. I do understand that Flo telling Sally she has been pretty much having an affair with me for the past month or so might result in some high drama, so I can wait a bit longer. And I'll try not to let it get to me. When I meet her after school I don't give her a hard time. I just hug her, tell her everything is fine, and walk with her to her house. It will all be OK in the end.

Flo's kitchen is gorgeous. It's big with a long wooden table and all the cupboards are white wood. It could probably do with being repainted and the windows are a bit grubby, but still, it's a real family kitchen – or at least it looks like one.

'I'm really jealous of your house,' I tell her as I gorge

135

on the banana and chocolate spread sandwich she just made me. 'Mine is so boring. Nana and Pop don't ever buy anything new and everything is functional. Ya know? Plastic, so it's easy to clean and cheap so it doesn't matter if it breaks. Your parents at least have taste.' I stop eating, my mouth is full. 'Shit, sorry. I mean they had . . . no, they did . . .' My brain is finding it as hard to find the right words as my mouth is finding it to say them while stuffed with food. Flo tells me to shut up, kindly stopping me from digging the hole I am falling into.

The doorbell rings.

'Wait there. That'll be the childminder with Abi.' She goes out to open it and I hear them chatting in the hallway. I move over to the counter and start scooping out the chocolate spread with my finger. Just as I dip my finger deep into the pot the back door swings open. I jump and drop the jar of spread on the floor. I stick my finger covered in chocolate into my mouth and crouch down to pick up the jar. I look up, my finger still deep in my mouth. It's him.

'Always greet men on your knees, do you?'

I suck my finger as hard as I can and pull it out of my mouth. Why am I on the floor? Oh yes, the jar. I pick it up and pull myself up to standing. He is surprisingly close to me. His face has smears of black on it, his hair is a mess. His T-shirt is ripped in places and his jeans are filthy.

He is gorgeous.

'What are you sucking?'

'Excuse me?'

'Your finger. What are you sucking off your finger?'

136

I feel disgusting. I am stealing his chocolate spread and then dipping my licked finger back into the pot. Why am I so gross?

He takes my hand. My arm is like a dead weight, my face tight from the horror of being caught. He holds my hand up to his nose. 'Mmmm, Nutella.' His hand wraps around my fist like a bear's paw. I swallow the lump of chocolate that is still in my mouth as his tongue slides out and licks the full length of my finger. Then he closes his mouth around it and sucks slowly before he lets it drop back towards my body like a broken pendulum in a grand-father clock. 'I love chocolate spread,' he says, his eyes still burning a hole in my brain.

He taps his finger on the end of my nose and carries on walking through the kitchen. The spot where he touched me feels heavy, and my tongue instinctively tries to reach it, without much success. I pinch my arm hard. Yup, that really happened.

'Come on, Abi. Come and meet Renée.' Flo is back.

There is now a child in front of me. Cute as she is, she's a lot less exciting than Julian. I haven't moved.

'What's wrong? You look like you just got hit on the head with a brick,' says Flo.

Oddly, that is exactly how I feel. Minus the pain, but definitely as disoriented. I shake my face.

'Sorry, I was miles away. Thinking about the exams.'

Flo gives me an understandable look of confusion. Me saying I am thinking about exams is as unlikely as her saying she is joining the army.

'OK, well, exams aside for a minute. This is Abi, my little sister. Say hello to Renée, Abi.'

'Hello, Renée,' she says, her sweet face beaming up at me like a Disney Princess. She's the most perfect little girl I have ever seen, with her short brown hair, olive skin and tiny button nose.

'Hello, Abi. Lovely to meet you.' I extend my hand so she can shake it, but instead she charges at my legs and throws her arms around them, hugging me so tight I nearly fall over. I reach down to cuddle her back.

'Nice being adored, isn't it?' says Flo.

It really is.

Up in Flo's room I'm snooping through all of her drawers and scanning her wardrobe while she and Abi look at books on the bed.

'You're very nosey, Renée,' Flo says, as I yank open her underwear drawer and have a look inside.

'You're so tidy. Everything is all folded and neat. Does your mum do that?'

'No, I do it. Mess stresses me out. I spend so much time clearing up after this little monkey that I automatically keep my own stuff tidy. Get out of my knicker drawer,' Flo orders.

I close it. Its contents aren't hugely insightful.

'Do you ever wear G-strings?' I ask casually.

'What, the ones that go up your bum? No way. Do we have to talk about this in front of Abi?'

'Sorry.' I carry on pottering around. Flo has lots of little tins full of things like hair clips and safety pins. At her dressing table there is a drawer full of make-up, none of which I can imagine her wearing. Red lipsticks and blushers, that sort of thing.

'Most of that is Mum's. She dumps the stuff she can't fit in her own room in here. Just one more way to invade my space,' Flo says, smiling, as if Abi won't know that she is complaining about her mother if she grins as she says it.

'Do you ever get on with her?' I ask, intrigued by their relationship.

'Never. She isn't interested in me, I'm not interested in her. We've both given up trying. But as long as this one is happy,' she lifts Abi's chin with her fingers and kisses her forehead, 'then who cares really. WAIT, what are you doing with that?'

Her shift of tone makes me jump and I almost drop the wooden box I am holding. 'B-B-blast!' I say, trying not to swear in front of Abi. 'What was that about? What's in here, a dead body?'

Her eyebrows meet her hairline, and making sure Abi is looking away she mouths, 'DAD.'

I feel like I'm holding a bomb. A bomb made of dead people. I lean backwards as I extend my arms and hand it to her. She takes it and puts it on the bed.

'It's OK, you are allowed to be freaked out,' Flo reassures me.

'Oh my God oh my God oh my God oh my God.' I rub my hands on my thighs. 'I am so sorry. I didn't think that he . . . it . . . they would be in your bedroom. Why are they . . . is he . . . it . . . . in your bedroom?'

'Because no one else in this house cares about them, and Da—' She stops herself when she realises Abi is trying to work out what we're talking about. '*He* deserves better than that.'

'Well, what are you going to do with them? You can't just leave them in here. Is your mum going to scatter them somewhere?' I ask, hoping she has some sort of plan.

Her face drops, in the way that it does sometimes. It goes from normal to heartbroken in under a second, reminding me that even though she tries to hide it, she is really sad.

'No, and neither is Julian. They don't think it's important. As far as they are concerned he's gone, and that is that.'

'What's in that box?' asks Abi.

'Nothing, it's just my bits and pieces,' Flo says with a fake smile.

'Then why did Renée scream?'

'I am just very silly,' I tell her, and I join them on the bed. Flo and I both pretend to read Abi's books. The silence is awkward.

'Do you think your dad would ever have jumped off the wall?' I ask as my mind fills with ideas.

'WHAT? No, he would never have done that to us.' She puts her hands over Abi's ears. 'Renée, what the hell? My dad didn't and wouldn't kill himself. He was better than that.'

'No, I don't mean to *kill himself*,' I say quickly. 'I mean for fun. Do you think he would have been the type of person to jump off the wall at Havelet, like we did? Did he ever do that?'

She looks sorry for thinking the worst of me.

'No, he never did it. But back in the day, when he was happy, he would have loved to have done it, I'm sure. He was that kind of person.'

'Then I think he should do it. Now, with us. We can take Abi. We don't have to jump, but we can let him do it. What do you think?' I ask.

'You mean throw . . . *the box* off the wall? Scatter his ashes in the sea? Now?' She takes a moment to think. 'Will you really come with me?'

'Of course I will. Right now. Let's do it before it gets too late. Do you want to come on an adventure with us, Abi?'

'Yeeeaaaayy! An adventure!' Abi says as she jumps off the bed.

We put on some warm clothes and go downstairs. Before we leave I see Julian's feet in the living room, resting on the coffee table. Next to them, a girl's feet. I feel a pang of jealousy, but bury it. We have something important to go and do.

Flo

By the time we've walked through town and reached the wall, the sky is well and truly black. An almost full moon

141

with the Christmas lights from nearby restaurants gives us enough light to see clearly, but the air is freezing. Abi seems happy to be tagging along, but I get a sudden sense that what we are doing is wrong.

'I shouldn't be doing this. I know Mum and Julian are what they are, but this doesn't feel right.'

'Look, you say neither of them cared about him when he was alive, and that neither of them cares about him now, so what's the problem? He's *your* dad, yours and Abi's. You two are the only people who loved him enough to do this properly,' Renée says as she decides which part of the wall to sit on.

I think back to the funeral. The chapel full of people who meant so little to me, Mum and Julian's indifference, Aunty Ada's short-lived attention to his life. Those colleagues who were there because they felt obliged. Renée is right. Abi and I are the two people who love him most.

'But should she be with us?' I say, nodding my head towards my little sister. We stop walking and Renée turns to me. She looks serious.

'I wasn't allowed to go to my mum's funeral, and one day Nana and Pop put on fancy outfits and came back a few hours later saying that the ashes had been spread, and that she was completely gone. Done. Not to be mentioned again. The last time I saw my mum I was pulled out of the room by Pop because she was coughing so hard she was sick. Pop told me she needed some space and I never saw her again. I used to sit with her all day long and make her laugh, then someone decided that me being there was wrong and dragged me away from her when she needed me there the most. She didn't even notice me leaving.' Renée swallows hard. I can see that she is trying not to cry. She takes a breath, blows it out quickly, and carries on. 'Now I'm old enough to understand everything, and the fact that I didn't get to hold her ashes, or say goodbye to her, makes me so angry. Angry with Pop for taking over and not letting me say goodbye properly, and angry with Nana for not being stronger and making spreading her ashes about all of us and not just them. Abi might not understand what is going on now but one day she will thank you for letting her be here for this. She will, I promise.' She holds the box up so it is level with our faces. 'Your dad is in here, he's still in here. You guys have to say goodbye to him now.'

She hands me the box. I feel so sad. Renée had never told me about what happened to her mum in such detail. It's all so heartbreaking.

'I'm so sorry about your mum. I don't know what it feels like to watch someone get so ill.'

'Don't worry about me. We're here for your dad tonight. I'm fine,' Renée says in a really grown-up voice.

'You don't have to tell me you're fine. I'm not fine. You're not fine either. We can be honest with each other about that, can't we?' I say. The sides of her face tense as she tries to stop herself from crying, but she can't.

There is something about her grief that makes mine less exclusive. Less like my world isn't the only one falling apart. Sally doesn't know about grief so she has no sympathy for it, and girls like Carla and Gem have no idea what it feels like for families to be broken, but Renée and I do. We both know how it feels to have the worst thing imaginable happen. I know it now – scattering Dad's ashes with Renée and Abi is absolutely the right thing to do.

We go and sit on the wall. The tide is in so the fall isn't high but still Renée keeps Abi on her lap and holds onto her as tightly as she can. I have the box, along with some last-minute nerves.

'Just imagine him standing here like we did, and how much he would love to have jumped in,' says Renée, as she puts her hand on my back.

Warm tears slide down my cold face. I hold the box in both hands and bring it to my lips, I kiss it.

'You might not really understand this now, Abi. And you might not remember this all when you grow up, but remember that Dad loved you more than anything. And even after I do this, he still always will,' I tell her.

She seems to know what the box represents, even if she doesn't know exactly why.

I look at Renée. Her tears are coming more heavily than mine. 'Go on,' she says. 'Please just do it.'

I hold the box up to my face.

'Thank you for being my dad,' I whisper. 'You were the best.'

I turn the box to face the sea. As I open it a gust of wind comes from behind us and takes its contents with it. The grey dust is lit up by the night sky as it falls onto the sea below us, and I throw the box in after it. It floats in the moonlight like risen treasure from a sunken ship. We watch it as the tide carries it out to sea. The impulse to scream takes over me.

'I LOVE YOU, DAD. I LOVE YOU.'

Abi reaches her arms out and carefully moves onto my lap. I wrap my arms around her to keep her warm. Renée drops her head onto my left shoulder. We stay like this until the box is swept away, and out of sight.

Dad is gone.

7

The Most Wonderful
Time of the Year?

Renée

*Hey babe, want to come over to Gem's tonight for
a bit of Christmas love? Just us. What's on your list
this year? We have asked for loads of clothes. Fingers
crossed!!!*
Come tonight?
Carla and Gem x

I don't know why they bother with the 'fingers crossed'
bit. There hasn't been a Christmas in history that they
haven't got everything they asked for. I'm like a homeless
kid in a movie at Christmas, walking the streets and
watching families through windows being all happy and
celebrating with tables and tables of gorgeous food. Our
Christmas Day is quite different. We get one present and

it's really just a Sunday lunch with party hats and turkey instead of chicken, which is literally the most boring meat ever and always so dry that I need a swig of water with every mouthful to get it down my neck. I'd much rather have a tin of Chicken in White Wine Sauce instead. No one wants to do anything other than watch the TV in our house, so that is pretty much all we do all day long. Unlike Carla and Gem's families, who play games and take hours over opening all their amazing presents. I have to block their voices out when they tell me about it because it makes me really sad.

I get to Gem's house at about 8 p.m. The driveway is glowing with fairy lights and Christmas decorations. It's a winter wonderland. I try to imagine what it might be like to come home to a house like this every day after school in the run-up to Christmas, and then to walk in the door and for the house to smell like pine cones and the fridge to be full of food, everyone smiling and Christmas music playing. Carla's house is just the same. They both think this is normal.

'Helloooooo,' I shout as I walk in the door.

'Renée! So good to see you. Happy Christmas and welcome.' Gem's dad leads me into the kitchen, where everyone else is.

'Renée, YAAAAAY!' say Carla and Gem at the same time.

There's Carla and Gem, their boyfriends Adam and Mark, and Gem's mum. I hadn't expected their boyfriends

147

to be here so I instantly feel like a gooseberry and my mood crashes. Almost as soon as I walk in I want to get out.

'Renée has been AWOL. We think she's got a new boyfriend,' says Gem suggestively.

A chorus of 'Ooooooooo' fills the room.

'No, honestly, I've just been concentrating on school-work,' I tell them, hoping to end that conversation.

'PAHAHHA, good one,' says Carla. 'You never concentrate on schoolwork. It's a booooooyyyy.'

'No. Honestly, I haven't get a new boyfriend.' I turn to Gem's mum. 'The house looks lovely, Mrs Gardner.'

'Well, you have to make an effort at Christmas, don't you? I am sure your grandparents have the place looking super too,' says Gem's mum. There's an awkward silence. 'Right then. We'd better be off,' she continues. 'Have fun, all of you. ONE glass of wine each, OK? Oh, and Renée, I keep meaning to call your grandmother to ask her, but can you bring Gem's white jeans with you next time? You've had them for a while.' She says it nicely, but she gives me a weird look.

'OK, Mum,' says Gem. 'GO. God, why are parents SO embarrassing? Go. GO!' Gem ushers them out of the door.

Mr and Mrs Gardner think this is hilarious. They leave.

'So is it just us then?' I ask.

'Yup, just us and loads of wine,' says Gem as she pours herself a huge glass and then gives Adam the kind of Frenchie I thought only happened in films. Carla is sitting with her legs wrapped around Mark, and I feel like the

148

world's biggest lemon sitting on my own on a kitchen chair. I used to feel like this all the time and it didn't bother me, but it's different now.

'So seriously, where have you been? We haven't seen you in months. You disappear after school every day and we never see you at the weekends. Who is your secret?' Gem takes a huge swig of wine then hands it to Adam for some totally unnecessary glass sharing.

'No one. Things have just been really tough at home. Things are hard, that's all.'

I know this is a slight fabrication but I have promised Flo I'd keep quiet about us, and besides, I want to test them. I have been the third wheel in this friendship for around ten years. They have no idea who I really am. It's the exact opposite to my friendship with Flo. All these years I've passed off their lack of interest in me as an innocent vacancy, but it's now feeling more like selfishness. I don't belong here.

'Yeah,' I continue. 'Nell is really sick. She's anorexic. Pop is getting angrier and angrier. Nana is showing signs of madness, I'm sure of it. I share a room with a person who hates my guts, I'm not allowed to watch the TV shows I want to watch and the food I get given is generally burnt or out of date. All in all being at home is really shit and I hate my life.'

Silence.

More silence. Except for an occasional awkward laugh from one of the boys.

'Right . . .' says Carla. 'Um, well, at least it's Christmas,

149

right? You can all have a really nice time and then 1995 will be a whole new year and you guys can make everything better.'

'Yes, I am sure your grandpa is just upset because it's so cold,' Gem says dimly.

'No, Gem, he isn't upset because it is cold. He is upset because my mum died of cancer and lumbered him with me and Nell, who is starving herself because she hates herself so much. I wake up every day in the room that my mum died in after spending the night dreaming about her in various states of her illness. Considering all that, I really don't think anything is going to improve when the sun comes out, do you?' I say with an intense stare.

They look at each other for support. Neither of them even thinking to support me. There is more silence.

'Well, this has all got a bit depressing, hasn't it?' says Adam finally, in his big, dumb, posh voice. 'Shall we all get pissed and move on?'

A round of wine is poured and some crisps are emptied into a bowl. I am acting out of character and I'm not quite sure where it's come from. I didn't plan this.

'So what are you asking for for Christmas then?' asks Gem nervously, clearly unsure of how I will respond and equally as unsure of how she will cope if I carry on with more depressing stories about life outside of My Little Pony Land.

'I don't do a Christmas list. It feels a bit mean when Nana and Pop have so little money. Not everyone can have what they want,' I say, being deliberately snide.

150

They all flinch at my snarky remark and just for a moment I feel bad. They have asked me over for a fun Christmas party and I am throwing this stuff at them out of nowhere. Spending time with people who only want a version of me is exhausting though, and it's making me angry.

'Renée, babe, not being funny, but it's Christmas and this is all a bit of a downer,' offers Carla. 'We should all just have some fun. I'm sure everything with your family will work out in the end.'

My friendship with them makes no sense. I get up.

'I'm going to go. You guys don't have the brain space for anyone else and I am a bit tired of trying to get you to notice me.'

'Bloody hell, someone's ego thinks it should be the centre of attention,' guffaws Adam.

'Yeah, Renée. Carla and I are best friends. We don't mean to leave you out, but we are *best* friends,' says Gem.

'I know,' I say, 'and you're lucky to have each other, but I don't want to be your tag along any more. It makes me feel like shit. I don't want to ruin your Christmas, I just felt I had to be honest with you.'

As I get to the door I hear Carla say, 'She's just in a bad mood. She'll get over it.' Then they carry on talking about something else.

I walk to Flo's house. All the lights are on so I brave her crazy mum and knock on the door, hoping she's home.

The door opens.

It's him.

Every time I see him words become a challenge and my heart pounds with fear, or panic, or something.

'Ahh, Little Miss Chocolate Fingers. Hello.'

I want to push my finger into his mouth. Have him suck it while I gaze into his eyes. *Be cool, Renée. Be cool.*

'Hello.'

Trying to act cool isn't easy when you feel like your heart is going to burst through your chest. 'Is, um, Florence home?' I have no idea why I just called her Florence.

He pauses. There is no need for it. He obviously knows the answer.

'No. She went to the cinema with that Sally girl. Want to come in and wait for her? I'm up in my bedroom.'

Did I hear him right? Is he joking?

'I . . . in, your . . .'

'I'm kidding, but she won't be much longer. Come and wait with me. I'll give you some Nutella. You like that, don't you?'

I follow him through into the kitchen like a dog on a lead, past the Christmas tree in the hall, which is surprisingly impressive, and into the kitchen. At the table I take a seat. He puts a pot of Nutella in front of me with a teaspoon in it.

'More licking, less sucking this time, don't you think?'

I can barely coordinate my hand to pick up the spoon. He sits next to me watching me, smiling, his eyes squinting. I feel like a mouse again, so small and squeaky, and he is big, like a bear. He could pick me up and ravish me with his mouth if he wanted to. I want him to. Why am I being so pathetic? He looks at my face like he wants to eat it.

'You not hungry?'

I realise I'm sitting still with a spoon full of Nutella in my hand, trying to take my eyes off his face.

'I can't swallow.'

He takes the spoon out of my hand and puts it to my lips. My mouth pops open and the spoon goes in.

'Lick it,' he says.

My tongue rigidly works the chocolate spread off the spoon and I gulp to get it down.

'That's it,' he says. He moves forward until his face is so close to mine that I could touch it with my tongue. His breath smells like chocolate and beer and the heat from his face makes my top lip wet. I worry he might hear my heart, it's beating so fast.

'You're very pretty,' he says, his lips now so close to mine that I can feel them move.

'Thanks,' I reply, breathy and shy.

'Can I kiss you?' he asks, but starts before I have the chance to answer. It's the softest, wettest kiss I've ever had. He pushes his tongue in past my lips and moves it perfectly around my mouth. I try to reciprocate but my tongue won't do what I want it to do so I stop trying and just let him kiss me. I barely notice his hand moving up my leg and into my knickers. Even if I wanted him to get off me I wouldn't be able to make him. I feel like my muscles have stopped working and there is no way

I can speak. He is kissing my mouth and all around my mouth, but I'm unable to kiss him back. I just take it, my jaw dropped open, my tongue hanging uselessly. Then I feel my body clench, my feet leave the ground and I fall forward like I'm wrapping myself around a ball. I know my cheeks are blushing, and my whole body is tingling. No one but me has ever made that happen before. I don't know what I am supposed to say or do. I don't want him to look at my face so I keep looking down.

He takes his hand away and pulls my skirt back over my legs.

'My turn,' he says, as he stands up and unzips himself.

My mouth is so dry it's hard to move my lips. Here? Now?

His hands are on the back of my head as he gently moves backwards and forwards. I don't have the confidence I've had when I've been drunk with other boys at parties. I'm sure that I'm doing it all wrong.

His groans get louder and quicker. His hands hold my head firmer with every thrust and then he comes. I haven't let anyone do that before and I don't like it. A small dollop trickles down my throat and makes me cough, another dollop smears across my cheek, the rest goes splat on the floor because I start gagging. I feel so embarrassed. I don't want him to look at my face.

'And there was me thinking you would know what to do,' he says, laughing. I feel like a mouse again.

'It took me a bit by surprise, that's all,' I say, wanting

154

to wipe my mouth but not knowing if I should or not.

He puts himself away and zips up his jeans. I rub in what hit the floor with my shoe and sit there. I feel unsexy and inexperienced.

The front door opens. Flo is home. There isn't time to do anything but sit up straight.

'Renée, what are you doing here?' Flo asks as she comes into the kitchen.

I can barely speak from the shame.

'I, I thought you might be home.'

'No, Sally made me go and watch some crap film then talked the whole way through it about some guy who apparently keeps coming over to their house and telling her how sexy she is. I wish I hadn't bothered,' Flo says, obviously annoyed.

Julian is at the fridge drinking out of a Sunny Delight bottle. He winks at me behind Flo's back. I still haven't processed what just happened.

'What's that on your cheek?' asks Flo, so close to me that she steps on the wet patch on the floor.

I put my hand up to my face. Some tiny flakes come away in my hand.

'Yoghurt,' I spurt. 'It must have been there since Carla and Gem's. When I was there I had a yoghurt. Strawberry. A strawberry yoghurt.'

'Here you go, wipe it off with this.' She wets a piece of kitchen roll under the tap and passes it to me. 'Shall we go to my room?'

'Sure,' I say, feeling like I just swallowed a chair.

As I follow her out of the kitchen Julian grabs my arm. 'Next time wear those white jeans.'

Next time?

Flo

Christmas, I can tell you, is not something I have been looking forward to for so many reasons. Least of all because the 25th of December is also my birthday.

I used to think the reason Mum hated me so much was because I ruined Christmas for her in 1978. She's never held back on the details of my 'horrendous' birth. Apparently getting me out was a military operation that took two midwives, a huge incision and a pair of forceps. There are very few pictures of me as a baby because my head was so wonky that Mum didn't want pictures taken until I resembled a human baby rather than an alien from outer space. Luckily, Abi was a perfect bundle who just popped out so has been adored from the start. Makes you wonder how ugly I was, seeing that Mum loves me about as much as she loves cow pats.

The Christmas holidays are even worse this year because I'm grounded. Abi enthusiastically told Mum about our little adventure down at Havelet, and although Mum doesn't seem to care why we were there in the first place, she is fuming with me for letting Abi get up on the wall. I've spent the days playing with Abi and the evenings studying. Our mock exams are coming up in January and

I need to do well in them. I really, really miss Renée though.

On the morning of the 25th there is a dull ache inside me from the moment I wake up at seven thirty. Dad always used to wake me up before anyone else got up, so that he could come into my room with a present before Christmas made everyone forget about my birthday completely. But there is obviously no chance of that this year. I lie in bed imagining him at the door.

Flo, Flo, Happy Birthday to Flo, Happy birthday to Flo, Happy Birthday to Flo, oh . . . Happy Birthday to Flo . . .

He'd have a present in his hand. Sometimes it was huge, sometimes tiny. Last year it was a satchel I wanted for school with a really cool T-shirt in it. The present was always wrapped in birthday paper rather than Christmas paper, and the card was always just from him saying something like, *Stupid Christmas. I love your birthday the best.*

Today, when I go downstairs there is a single envelope on the kitchen table with my name on it. Inside it is a card saying *Dear Flo, Many Happy Returns, Mum, Fred, Julian and Abi.* Next to it is a present. It's wrapped in Christmas paper but has a Happy Birthday rosette on it. It's small and soft, obviously something to wear. For a few seconds I get excited about a cool new top, or some jeans, or maybe a new denim jacket. But it isn't, it's a pair of pink Marks and Spencer's pyjamas.

I make myself a cup of tea and then go back to my

room, put on my new pyjamas and get into bed. At eight thirty Abi comes in and jumps on me, and I take her downstairs to start opening her presents. The fact that it is my birthday isn't mentioned again for the rest of the day. Fred cooks lunch.

'I love a nice moist bird,' he says as he pulls the turkey out of the oven. Mum does a slutty laugh.

He takes his seat at the head of the table, where Dad used to sit. Julian is at the other end, Mum and Abi on one side, me on the other. The middle of the table is covered in small bowls of different dishes. Brussels sprouts with bacon, cranberry sauce, roast potatoes, parsnips with parmesan cheese – to be fair to Fred, he is a really good cook, but I still hate him.

'So Flo, how is the revision going?'

Being asked a direct question by Fred is uncomfortable for me, especially as I have an audience. The world's most critical audience.

'All right,' I reply.

'And what subjects are you doing for GCSE?'

The fact that this man is living in my house and doesn't know what I'm studying for my GCSEs is everything I have a problem with. Who is he? Were he and Mum seeing each other while Dad was still alive? Is he the real reason Dad was so depressed? I hate that I'm expected to just accept him. Maybe the old Flo would have done, but not any more. I've had enough of being the one who feels like crap all the time because of everyone else.

'You know, just cos you are screwing my mother doesn't

158

mean we need to be friends,' I say, staring him right in the eye.

'NO.' Mum stands up, her face looking haggard. 'Get out. GET OUT. I don't want you at this table this Christmas. Your room. NOW.'

I take a moment to load some more food onto my plate. 'Abi, come up and watch *Pingu* with me in a bit, yeah?'

'She will do no such thing,' Mum says, sitting down hard onto her chair.

I take my plate and go upstairs. I spend the rest of my birthday alone, and for that reason I actually have quite a nice time.

Renée

I have thought about nothing but Julian since that night in Flo's kitchen. Every door I open I imagine him behind it, every street I walk down I plan what I will say if he is on it. Nothing Pop, Nell or Nana says is enough to take the smile off my face. I'm like a dog with a bone. My thoughts and fantasies are as far as my eyes can see. Even my appetite has completely gone. That is how I know I'm in love.

It's the way he touched me. I thought I knew about boys – how to touch and be touched, but I knew nothing of how good it could feel until him. Before him it was all for show. Experimenting just for practice really. Julian knew exactly what to do, there was no showing off. I just need to do it again, this time to get it right. Next time I will do it better and show him that I can be perfect too.

'Eat your turkey,' orders Pop when he catches me gazing out of the window. If he had any idea of what I am imagining in my head he would throw me out of the house and never let me come back. I cut a small piece of turkey, squash it onto a fork with a soft Brussels sprout and swallow it with a big gulp of water. The only thing I can taste is salt.

Nell is now openly not eating food. Nana and Pop must be realising the seriousness of her situation because they never tell her to eat up. They know that whatever it is she's going through is well beyond anything they can cope with, so they just watch her as she becomes thinner and thinner, none of us knowing where it will all end up, all of us hoping that one day she'll pick up a piece of toast and eat it without cutting it into twenty pieces and making it last half an hour. I think Nell needs to see a doctor, but that would involve someone admitting that there was a problem, and I have no hope for that happening anytime soon. Sometimes I want to tell Nana and Pop to make her eat, but if I have learned anything living in this house, it's that I should just stay quiet.

'Shall we do presents now?' asks Nana when we have finished our Marks and Spencer's Christmas pudding. Her enthusiasm, at least, makes us all smile.

After we all watch Nell open hers – a pair of hair crimpers – it's my turn. 'This is for you, Renée. We know you wanted it last year, but here it is now.'

Oh my goodness. Is this the bomber jacket that I had admired in town with Nana last year when we were uniform shopping? I had picked it up off a rail in Pandora and told her that I liked it, but it was £30. I hoped that she would go back and get it, and that she would give it to me for Christmas, but on the day I was given a checked flannel shirt instead. Can she possibly have saved up all year for the jacket? Is this about to be the best present ever? I unwrap it like Charlie unwrapped the Wonka Bar that had the golden ticket inside. Everyone's eyes are ready to capture my reaction.

Long pause.

'Well, what do you think?' urges Nana.

'It's a shellsuit,' I say slowly.

Nell laughs for the first time in weeks.

'Yes, I remember when all the girls were wearing them and we couldn't afford one for you. Well, as it is your GCSEs this year, Pop and I thought you deserved something a bit special.' Nana smiles at me.

I hold the top between the thumb and forefinger of each hand and raise it up in front of me. It's purple with white and neon stripes on the arms. It's disgusting.

She is right, shellsuits had been all the rage, three years ago. I had cried because I wasn't part of the phenomenon that lasted all of a month, because after everyone's initial bout of madness, we all realised quite quickly that aside from being major fire hazards, they are one of the most repulsive items that the 90s ever created. Shellsuits are now only mentioned in sentences like 'She is so sad, I bet

161

she wears shellsuits' and here I am with a brand-new one.

'Go on, Renée, put it on for us all to see,' smirks Nell.

'Yes. Put it on to show your nana,' says Pop, not taking his eyes off the TV.

I walk out of the room and go up to the bathroom. How am I going to pretend like this?

I stand looking at my reflection in the bathroom mirror. Even with mascara and lip gloss it is impossible to make a shellsuit look attractive. Aside from the fact that it is undeniably comfortable and its lightweight fabric makes me feel like I'm floating, it is hideous. If anyone beyond these four walls ever sees me wear it then any street cred I've managed to establish over the last fifteen years will be crushed. This. Is. Awful.

I go back downstairs and push open the door to the lounge. I think my eyes might be closed.

'It's perfect,' gushes Nana. 'It fits you perfectly. I am so pleased.'

'Yup, that's a good solid outfit there, Renée. Will last you years,' adds Pop.

'That is one hand-me-down I can't WAIT for,' gleams Nell, sarcastically.

'It's perfect for around the house,' I say. It's the only positive sentence I can muster.

I sit myself on the sofa and peel a satsuma. I can't wait for the new term to start.

162

8

A Spanner in the Works

Renée

On the coldest, darkest morning of the winter so far I am up and out the house so fast the rain hardly touches me. We are back to school, and I can't wait to see Flo. I've missed everything about our friendship. Our conversations, our notes, our after-school chips and then of course, her brother. I wonder if he has mentioned me at all, if he's told her over the holidays that he is in love with me and that he is planning on asking me to be his girlfriend. How amazing would that be? Flo as my best friend and her cool, sexy, gorgeous older brother as my boyfriend. At some point Julian will tell Flo everything, and he will tell her not to be mad with me for loving him, and she will be happy for me and everything will be fine.

When Sally isn't looking I grab her fountain pen and throw it under Miss Anthony's desk. As she scrambles around for it I launch a note at Flo.

163

AHGAH, I missed you so much. Soossososooso sosososo much! How was Christmas? Mine was SHIT. So glad to be back at school. I didn't do any revision for the mocks though, did you? I'll do some last minute cramming this week. How are yyooouuuuu?? Shall I come to your house after school?
R x

She manages to reply before Sally gets back to her seat.

I missed you toooo!!! Christmas was rubbish, but I did revise loads so I guess that's good. YES, lets meet up after school but not at my house. We can get the bus to Vazon Bay and sit in the cafe? Anywhere but home! See you at the end of the lane x x

OK, so he obviously hasn't told her yet.

We arrive at Vazon, a long sandy beach on the west coast of the island, at 4 p.m. The sky is getting dark but the rain is holding off. Even I have given into the warmth of a duffel coat now. It's really cold. We run from the bus stop to the cafe but forget to slow down when we get to the door. We burst in and skid on our wet feet then fall over and land in a heap on the cafe floor. Flo takes a stand full of postcards down with her and lies there giggling so much she can't get up. She reaches out for me to help her up but I'm too floppy from laughing and can't help her. This makes her laugh even more so she has to hold herself

164

between the legs to stop herself weeing. But then she stops laughing, her face turns pure white, and a look of fear moves over her face.

'What? Did you actually wee?' I ask.

She shakes her head slowly. I realise there is someone standing behind me.

'Wow, now you look cool,' says a voice I recognise. 'Last time I saw you, you were lying down bleeding all over the ground, now you are lying down trying not to wet yourself. What a lady!'

It's Samuel Franklin, sitting at a table with some other surfer boys. They're all laughing at Flo on the floor. They all obviously know about the period-under-the-bush incident.

'What's your problem, Samuel?' I say, turning to him and his ugly friends.

'Ooooooooooo,' they smirk, like five-year-olds.

'Seriously, what is your problem? You think a girl having a period is hysterical, do you? Well, do you know what I think? I think you are the worst kisser I've ever kissed. You lick teeth like a little lizard. If I had to choose between kissing you and being covered in Flo's period, I'd take the period any day.'

All of his mates laugh. Samuel shifts uncomfortably. Flo gets up and stands behind me.

'What are you, like, lesbians or something?' he says, trying to look cool.

'With boys like you around it's a surprise we're not all lesbians. And anyway, everyone at Tudor Falls thinks you're

165

gay,' I say proudly. What's a little white lie when you have a friend to protect?

As the lady who works in the cafe gets down onto her hands and knees to pick up all of the beach balls and postcards that Flo took with her when she fell, I shove three packets of Wotsits and a £5.99 picnic blanket under my coat.

'I'm not gay,' says Samuel to his friends.

'You're so gay,' they repeat back to him.

I pull Flo outside.

Down on the beach we huddle into a dug-out section of the huge grey wall, wrap the blanket around us and open all of the crisps.

'No one has ever stuck up for me like that before. Ever,' says Flo with her hand inside a crisp packet.

'Well, Samuel is a prick and you are my best friend. There is no way I'm letting a boy humiliate you like that. No way.'

'Sally would have given him a round of applause,' Flo says under her breath.

'Yeah, well, like I have said a million times, Sally is an idiot. And as soon as you pluck up the courage to tell her about us then the sooner you can realise that friends are not supposed to treat each other that way.' I stuff six Wotsits into my mouth so I don't have to keep talking.

'I've never trusted anyone the way I trust you,' Flo says. 'Well, apart from Dad, obviously. You act like you care about me as much as you care about yourself sometimes. I can't get used to it.'

'Well, it's true.' I want to tell her about Julian, but not now. This isn't the right moment. We look out to sea as we eat our Wotsits.

'Shall we be blood sisters?' I say, our bodies huddled close under the blanket, our breath frozen.

'Huh? You can't just become someone's sister. Well, not unless you marry their brother and if you ever do that I'd kill you,' Flo laughs.

I try not to react.

'No, blood sisters,' I tell her. 'I read it in a book once. Two best friends pricked the ends of their fingers and then pressed them together so their blood combined and that made them blood sisters. Then they made a promise to be best friends forever and there was no going back after that, they were bound.'

'What will we cut our fingers with?' she asks nervously.

I dig beneath my duffel coat and pull a safety pin from the hem of my school skirt. 'This?'

Flo's not convinced.

'Come on,' I say. 'It won't hurt. Much.'

I burn the end of the pin with my lighter.

'What are you doing that for?'

'I am sterilising it. It'll stop us getting infections.' I press the needle into the soft cushiony bit of my forefinger and a small dot of blood blobs out. It hurts, but not much. My finger is pretty numb from the cold. 'OK, your turn.'

'Renée, I don't think I want to do this. What about AIDS?' Flo says, looking very worried.

167

'You think I have AIDS?'

'Well, I don't know. Do you know you haven't got it?'

'Flo, only gay people get AIDS,' I say, unsure of whether that is true or not.

'No, anyone can get it. There was a girl in Guernsey last year who was caught dripping her blood into all the men's pints in a pub. Someone caught her and it turned out she had AIDS and was getting back at men. Anyone who has sex can have AIDS.'

I suck my finger. I vaguely remember that story.

'Well, I've never had sex, and I'm pretty sure you can't get it from blow jobs.' I feel disappointed. Not just because I'm sitting here in the freezing cold with a hole in my finger, but because Flo thinks I might have AIDS.

'Don't be offended, Renée. I just don't think sharing blood is a good idea these days. Can we be spit sisters instead?' She puts her arms around me and presses her face up towards mine. 'Come on. Let's do it. Spit sisters.' She spits on her finger and holds it in front of me. 'Come on. Same thing, just spit. It's still from inside us.'

I reluctantly spit on the index finger that isn't bleeding and hold it up to hers. We press them together and close our eyes.

'I promise to be honest, and kind, and never to let you down,' says Flo, her finger pressing hard on mine.

'I promise to look after you, and stick up for you and not let anybody laugh at you,' I say, opening my eyes a little to check she has hers shut.

'I promise to be honest,' she says.

168

'I promise to be honest,' I repeat.

I wonder why I suggested such a pact, when I know that I've already blown it.

Flo

The best thing about sitting our mock exams is that in between them we have free periods where we can study whatever we need to study. Some people stay in Room Six, some go into the dining room, but Renée and I sneak into the library whenever we can because we can hide in one of the little alcoves and be together.

'What are you doing? You're not supposed to write in the books!'

'I am not writing in it. I am circling letters to make a code,' she says, defensively.

'What code?'

'Well, it isn't really a code. I'm circling the letters to spell swear words. Look.'

She turns the copy of *Great Expectations* towards me.

We (a)te the whole of the toast, and d(r)ank tea in preparation, and it is delightful to (s)(e)e (h)(o)w warm and greasy we al(l) get after it.

'See? *Arsehole*. Well, nearly. That sentence is missing an e for the end. Bummer. Ha ha. "Bummer", didn't mean to do that.' She laughs.

'Renée, do you ever do any actual work?' I say, genuinely worried about her.

'These are just the mocks. I'll do some before our proper GCSEs, obviously.'

'You'd better. You need at least five to stay at Tudor Falls. If you get under five you have to either get a job or go to the grammar school. You can't stay here if you don't do well enough. Doesn't that worry you?' I say.

'Of course it worries me. I'm not stupid. I've listened in class, I know the basics, and anyway, no one ever gets less than five. You have to really mess up to get less than five. I'll be fine.'

She takes *Great Expectations* back and starts circling letters again.

'*Boobies*. Ha ha, brilliant!'

I can't not laugh.

'So, I was thinking maybe I could come over after school one day this week?' Renée says. 'I haven't seen Abi in ages and I miss your chocolate spread sandwiches. Nana doesn't buy stuff like that.'

'Really? You want to come to my house? I spend my life wanting to get out of it. Why don't we go to yours?' I suggest, realising that I have never actually been there.

'Trust me, you don't want to come to mine. It's just so cold out and my uniform never dries properly by the morning because Pop is so tight with the central heating. At least it's warm at yours, and I can come on a day when your mum is out.' She closes *Great Expectations* and crosses her arms. Is she really that desperate for a Nutella sandwich?

'OK, fine. Come to my house. If you come Friday then Mum and Fred won't be there.'

'Cool, I'll go home first to get changed and meet you there,' she says, opening up the book again and circling more letters.

I'm not sure why she thinks she needs to go home first, but before I get the chance to question it, the library fills with the sound of Sally's voice.

'Shit, shit shit shit shit shit,' I say as I duck down.

'NO, get out from under the table,' barks Renée, firmly. 'Lets face up to her now. Get out from under there.'

'Renée, I can't. Shit shit shit, I can't.'

'Well, if she sees you I'm telling her about us. And just so you know, your bum is sticking out and she is —'

'Flo, what are you doing under that table?' It's Sally.

I crawl out. Climbing up the chair like a child making its way to the naughty step.

'Why are you in here? With her?' Sally's face is red and veiny.

Renée sits up straight and crosses her arms. Her face looks proud as punch. She's been looking forward to this moment. 'We came in here to do revision together. Do you have a problem with that?' she says.

Come on, Flo. Be tough, be strong.

'Yes, of course I have a problem with that.' Sally looks at me. 'Renée Sargent is a twat and I don't want you hanging round with her. So why are you in here with her?'

'You're the twat, Sally,' blurts Renée, determined to win this battle.

'Shhhhhhhhhhhhhhhhhhhh. Silence in the library,' echoes Miss Le Hurray's voice. If this is going to happen, it is going to have to happen quietly.

171

'Sally,' says Renée, 'Flo is allowed to talk to whoever she wants, you know that, don't you? You don't own her.'

I am now sitting rigidly on the chair. My eyes may well be shut, I can't be sure. I prepare myself for flying pencil cases and equally as dangerous words.

'So, wait, are you guys friends now or something? Is that why you've been so full of yourself lately, Flo? Don't make me laugh. Flo, come with me. We need to revise French. You can stay with Renée if you like but you will fail everything and get a reputation for being a slut.'

'Don't go with her, Flo,' says Renée. 'Stay here. We have science prep to do.'

'I'll do the science prep with you, Flo. I am the set above you so I know all your stuff off by heart. Get your stuff together and come with me now.'

'No, Flo. Stay here. You don't have to do what she says,' says Renée firmly.

'Come.'

'Stay.'

'Come.'

'Stay.'

'OH, SHUT UP. SHUT UP, both of you. You're arguing over me like I'm a dog.'

'SILENCE IN THE LIBRARY! Who is that making that racket?' Miss Le Hurray appears like a little gremlin dressed in brown tweed. 'Renée Sargent, I should have known it would be you, but Sally and Florence, I thought better of you. Will anyone care to tell me what all this noise is about?'

'Nothing, miss. Flo is just saying how hard she has

172

found science this year. I am about to take her off for an intense lesson so I can help her with the exam tomorrow,' says Sally in her best lick-arse voice.

'Well, that is very generous of you, Sally. I'm sure Flo is very grateful. Gather your things together and go with Sally, Flo. Revision is very important for you all this year.'

Renée is silenced. Sally looks like the cat that got the cream. 'Come on, now!'

She storms to the door and waits.

'You're not going to go, are you?' asks Renée.

'But she is so mad. If I don't go she'll –'

Renée exhales loudly, throws down her pen and sits back. 'This is the moment we've been waiting for, Flo. She knows. Just leave her to go off in her strop, stay here with me.'

'I'm sorry. I can't.' I gather my things and meet Sally at the door.

'I told you before, if you become friends with Renée Sargent I'll make your life hell,' Sally growls.

'We were just doing some science revision. She isn't my *friend*,' I say, hating myself for lying.

'Good. Let's keep it that way. Now hurry up. I have to tell you about about Phil. I think it might get serious.'

Later, at lunchtime, I go looking for Renée. I see Margaret duck into the toilets and presume they are up to no good again so follow her in. 'Margaret, have you seen Renée?'

She nods her head to the left, gesturing at a toilet cubicle. I push it open and see Renée on her knees stretching a roll of cling film over the toilet bowl.

'Hey, I just wanted to say sorry about earlier. I feel awful and I . . .' I realise what she is doing. 'This was you guys too?'

I have just caught her in the act of the most annoying prank ever to be played at Tudor Falls. Unless you know it's there it is impossible to see the cling film when you sit on the toilet, so when you wee it sprays up and goes everywhere. I have been caught out by this twice. Of course it was the work of Renée and Margaret. Who else would find that funny?

'I just wanted to find you to say sorry,' I said again. 'I chickened out again and I feel really bad.'

She ignores me for a minute or two while she smooths out the cling film. When it's completely invisible she stands up and faces me. 'Any chance you could guide Sally this way? This one is for her.'

'I don't blame you for being annoyed. I will tell her. I will. It just has to be the right moment. You will still come to my house Friday, won't you?'

I expect to have to grovel more, but her face lights up when I ask about Friday. That apology was easier than I thought.

Renée

I've been sitting in the school hall for forty-five minutes staring at the page. Have we really learned this stuff in science class? Why don't I recognise any of it? The clock is moving so slowly. Everyone else around me is writing answers at a hundred miles an hour. I can't focus, and even if I could I don't know the answers. Daydreaming is my only option. In an hour and a half I will be at Flo's house. Hopefully Julian will be there. I'll have the white jeans on and act really cool. Keen enough to let him know how I feel but aloof enough to not look desperate.

But I am desperate. I am sooooo desperate. I have never wanted anything as much as I want him. I tick a few multiple choice answers and then wait. I'll revise before my real exam in a few months. This one really doesn't matter.

The bell rings. I'm out the door before anyone else has even left their seats. I need to get changed.

At home I run up the stairs and into my bedroom. Nell is lying on her bed, so frail and white. Just like Mum in this exact room eight years ago.

'Nell,' I whisper, because I'm finding it hard to breathe at the sight of her. 'Are you OK?'

'I can't do this any more, Renée. Living here, it's wrong.'

I don't want to do this now, I want to see Julian, but I sit next to her on her bed.

'I can help you,' I say.

'You can't help me. Of all the people *you* can't help me. You're the reason this is happening. You have no idea what it feels like to watch you being so happy all the time. I hate you for it,' Nell says, looking at me with total contempt.

'You think I'm happy? I think about Mum every day.'

'But you never show it. You've never tried to talk to me about it. You just carry on with your own life and forget about me,' she says bitterly.

I drop my head. How is this all my fault?

'There's no point being all sad about it now, Renée. It's too late for that.'

'But Nell, I tried . . .'

'No you didn't, you never tried. You acted like she was all yours. You had a week off school, when I was only allowed two days because everyone thought I didn't understand what was happening. You all carried on concentrating on yourselves while I tried to tell you all that I missed her more than anything else in the entire world, but you never wanted to listen.' She rolls over and faces the wall. 'Leave me alone, Renée.'

I get off her bed, squeeze myself into Gem's white jeans, and leave. I have two choices in life: I either try to do the right thing and get accused of being selfish, or I just do what is right for me and get called selfish anyway. This time, it's all about me.

'Look at you all dressed up,' says Flo as she opens the door.

'What? Really? These are the only things that fit me these days.' Nothing like a bit of self-deprecation to cover your tracks. 'Hey, Abi, how are you?'

'Renéeeeee!' She runs up to me and gives me one of her amazing cuddles. 'Will you play Lego with me?'

'Of course I will.' I take her by the hand into the living room.

176

'It's so nice having help with her. Can you keep an eye on her while I go and get our sandwiches?' says Flo.

'For sure. We're all good.'

In the living room Abi turns an entire box of Lego upside down.

'What are you going to build?' I ask.

'A new house for Fred.'

Flo raises an eyebrow as she walks in with two plates of sandwiches, clearly wishing Abi's house for Fred was real.

'So how was your science exam?' asks Flo.

'Not great, but it's fine. The real thing will be OK.'

'You need to start caring more, Renée. You'll fail everything,' Flo says like a teacher.

'All right! Bloody hell, is this have-a-pop-at-Renée-day or something?' I snap.

'God, sorry.'

We sit for a moment in an awkward silence.

'Who else has had a pop at you?' she asks eventually.

I tell her about Nell. How she says I could have made everything better if I had behaved differently. Flo squeezes my hand, and we both focus on Abi, who is building a really dodgy-looking house with her Lego.

'We were like her once. Clueless how people can let you down. Amazing to think there was a time where we thought someone would always be there to take care of us,' I say.

'I know, and I'm going to do everything I can to keep it that way for her. At least we have each other now, right?' Flo smiles.

177

I nod, my conscience not letting me look at her. Abi puts the last piece of Lego on the top of Fred's house. She looks pleased with herself.

'Now let's hope he lives in it,' grumbles Flo.

The peace is broken when the front door bursts open. I hear a girl giggle in the hallway, then I hear Julian's voice. My heart kicks off in a massive way.

'No, I have to go home. It's my mum's birthday,' says the girl.

We can see them through the gap in the door. The girl is now against a wall, Julian is against her.

'But I want you to stay here. I'll give you something nice to eat,' Julian says, smothering her face with his lips.

'I bet you will, but I have to go. Call me tomorrow. Next time, you drive. OK?'

She leaves.

'Gross,' says Flo. 'Sorry you had to see that. One of the million girls he has brought home this week.'

I try to hide my violent breathing. My gums tingle like they do after cross-country.

'Are you OK?' Flo gives me an odd look.

'Yep, yep, I'm fine. Just a lump of bread in my throat.'

Come on, Renée, you are cooler than this with boys.

Julian is now in the living room. He's covered in engine oil, his clothes are ripped. His face is dark with stubble. 'Hello, Abi. You built a house. Aren't you clever!'

'JULIAN!' Abi throws her arms around his legs, and he picks her up and holds her above his head. She giggles and giggles. I imagine she is our child, mine and his.

'OK, I need to go and have a shower. Where's Mum, Flo?' Julian asks.

'Don't ask me. She said she'd be back at six.'

He leaves. He didn't look at me once the entire time he was in the room. Did he not see me? Did he not recognise me? Is he playing hard to get? I hear the shower turn on upstairs. I think about him up there naked. Soap suds falling down his body. I close my eyes and imagine being in there with him, on my knees. Warm and wet, his hands on my head.

'Renée? Renée?'

I open my eyes.

'What's with you tonight?' asks Flo. 'You're being so weird.'

'Sorry,' I mutter. 'The Nell thing really threw me. I'm fine. Shall I make us a cup of tea?' I need to get out of the room for a minute.

'Sure.'

I stand trembling in the kitchen. My feelings are out of control. Poor Flo, she thinks I came to see her tonight and all I want to do is get off with her brother. The brother she hates, and who makes her feel like crap about herself. I am in love with him. What kind of best friend am I? I put two tea bags into cups and stand with my hands on the work surface, my head down. *Come on, Renée, don't do this. Don't do this to Flo.* And then I feel his hands on my hips.

'You wore the sexy jeans for me?'

He presses himself against me.

179

'Did you miss me?'

I answer with a super-speedy and mortifying nod. He turns me to face him. I move like a zombie. He's still wet, just a towel covering him from the waist down. His body is the most beautiful thing I've ever seen. I want to lick it. He smells of soap.

'Tell Flo you have to leave. I'll meet you at the end of the road in ten minutes. Would you like that?'

'Yes. Yes I'd like that.'

Zombie.

'Good. Ten minutes. Don't be late.'

He takes one of the cups of tea I've made and goes back upstairs.

'Here you go.' I pass Flo her tea. Guilt rising off me like steam from the cup.

'You not having one?'

'No. You know, I don't feel that great. I think I've eaten something, I haven't felt right all day,' I lie.

'I hope it wasn't my sandwich,' Flo says, worried.

'No, it wasn't your sandwich. Probably just a mix of not enough sleep and stress because of Nell and stuff. I'll be OK, but I should probably go.'

'Will you be OK getting home? The buses are only once an hour at this time.' She looks genuinely concerned for me.

'Yeah, I'll walk. The fresh air will do me good. See you over the weekend?' I say, feeling sick with guilt.

'Maybe. I need to do some revision, and Sally wants to go into town to buy a new coat, but call me and let's see,' Flo says, passing Abi another piece of Lego.

180

I fight the urge to ask her why the hell she is going shopping with Sally, and why she can't just tell her to go sod herself. But I hardly have the right to be righteous right now.

'Come on, get in.'

He pushes the passenger door open and I get in the car. It smells of stale cigarettes. He drives so quickly that I'm scared. I want to ask him to slow down but my fear of not looking cool is annoyingly overpowering. I hold onto the handle and close my eyes, opening them wide every now and then in case he looks at me. I don't want him to know I'm scared.

'Where are we going?' I ask as he drives too quickly down lanes I don't recognise.

'I know a good place. Somewhere private. That's what you want, isn't it? To be with me somewhere private?'

'Sure,' I say quietly.

'Sure? That doesn't sound very convincing.'

'No, I mean, yeah, I mean I want to do that. Private. Sure.'

Where has my personality gone?

Soon we are driving through town. I keep my head down in case anyone sees me in his car. I feel so conspicuous. I shouldn't be with him.

He races along the front of town and we pass Havelet Bay. I wonder if he knows that I helped spread his father's ashes there a few months ago. He certainly doesn't slow down or acknowledge it in any way. Then we start going up the Wiggly Woggly Road. I think of Mum coasting down it slowly, Nell and I laughing in the back. I would have fallen down if she had driven like this.

At the top he spins a sharp left and drives into Fort George, the 'Beverly Hills of Guernsey'. An estate where all the rich people from England buy houses, mansion after mansion with big expensive cars in the driveways. It's like another world and doesn't feel like Guernsey at all. He puts his foot down then screeches to an abrupt stop at the bottom of a hill. There is silence. We are in a little lay-by. Herm Island is right in front of us. The sky is dark, there is no one around. He gives me a cigarette.

'Thanks.'

We smoke without speaking. He sucks on his fag so hard that it makes a sound when he pulls it away from his lips, then he blows the smoke out of his mouth like he's trying to make it reach the moon. I am doing everything I can to be as quiet as possible. I don't want to do anything wrong. I want him to notice me without noticing me.

'Finished?'

'Yeah, I've finished.' I throw the fag butt out of the window and put my hands on my thighs. He turns to me.

'Have you done it before?'

'What, smoke? Of course I have!' How unexperienced does he think I am?

'No, not smoke. IT. Sex. Are you a virgin?'

I didn't think he'd bought me here for a nice chat, but sex? Are we really going to do it? I look at his face. He obviously isn't joking. Sex? In a car? Sober?

182

'Of course I'm not a virgin. I've done it.'

'Good.'

He turns the cog on the side of my seat so that it goes back, then he does the same with his. We are gently lit by a street lamp and the moon. Enough to see what to do, but not so bright he can see the details of my body. I can do this.

'Take off your jeans.'

I pull down the jeans and yank them over my feet. He undoes his too. I'm not scared, I'm not. I want this. His hand reaches over and pulls my knickers to the side.

'Do you want to go on top?' he asks.

'I don't mind.'

He leans over and opens the glove compartment, taking out an open packet of condoms. There is one left. I watch him as he rolls it on, glad he has thought to do this. I wouldn't have known how to bring it up if he hadn't.

He raises himself up and pulls himself over to my seat so he's on top of me. His face next to my face, his chest pressed against mine as he reaches down to guide himself inside me. I am ready. Flo will understand.

A sharp pain shoots up me as he crams himself in.

I take a deep breath and try to relax like he told me to. With one more thrust he is inside me. We both breathe a sigh of relief.

I cling onto his shoulders like he is rescuing me from the side of a cliff. If I let go I will fall. A few times I whimper when that sharp pain comes back, and each time he slows back down. I can tell he doesn't want to hurt me.

183

This isn't how I imagined it. I don't feel the pleasure I always thought I would feel when this moment came. It doesn't feel how it looks on TV. It's more like the time Margaret Cooper bet me to get my whole fist in my mouth. I am stuffed full. It feels as uncomfortable as it does unnatural. I feel nothing of the pleasure I felt in the kitchen. If it wasn't for his breath against my face, his tongue occasionally in my mouth, I might wonder what the point of sex is at all. Is it supposed to hurt like this?

His breath becomes shorter and he moves quicker, but I can tell he wants to go even faster than he is. His entire body flexes and he collapses onto me.

We lie still for a moment, my brain wondering, 'Is that it, is that it?'

That is it.

He pulls himself back over to his seat.

'You lied about being a virgin.'

I don't know how he knows, but there is no point in denying it.

'Sorry.'

'It would have been nice of you to have told me. I could get into trouble for shit like that. What are you, fifteen? You could say you changed your mind or something, and get me in a load of shit.'

I say nothing. I feel so stupid, so young, so silly.

He reaches to the back seat.

'Here, sit on this. I don't want you making a mess of my car.'

Unsure of what he means I pull up my jeans and push the plastic bag he gave me under my bum.

'OK, quick fag and then I better get you home.'

We smoke in silence, and then he starts the engine and drives off. This time much slower. This time I'm not so scared.

'Leave me here. It's fine, I'll walk up to my house,' I say as we get to the end of my road. I wonder if we will kiss goodbye, but he doesn't offer and I don't try. I stand by the car, and I lean back in through the open door.

'Thanks for the lift. I had a nice time.'

'Yeah. Renée?'

'Yes?' My heart thumps as I prepare to be launched to girlfriend status. 'Wrap your jacket round your waist when you go into the house.'

I close the door and he drives off. What did he mean about my jacket?

I look down and see a huge red stain on the crotch of Gem's white jeans.

Shame, panic, fear and a hundred other emotions hit me like a car. I pull off my coat and wrap it around my waist and make my way up to the house. Why? Why do things like this have to happen to me?

I open the front door as quietly as I can.

'Is that you, Renée?'

Obviously not quietly enough.

Pop's voice bellows from the living room. I can see them all watching the TV.

'Yes, Pop, I'll be down in a minute.'

I run up the stairs and into the bathroom, slamming the door shut and locking it before anyone has the chance to get in after me. In front of the mirror I see the horror of what I have done. Gem's white jeans ruined by the deep red ink of my virginity. How will I explain this?

I peel them off and run them under the cold tap, but as the pink water disappears down the plug hole I know trying to save them is pointless. I put them into the bath with my knickers.

In the mirror I look at my vagina. It feels red and sore – it's changed forever.

I open Mum's old drawer trying not to think about what it used to mean to me. I take out a tampon and put one foot up on the side of the bath. I slip the tampon's cardboard tube halfway inside me, and a gentle push has it double up and come away in my hand like I've been using them for years. The fear of entering that unknown space now gone. I feel proud of myself, grown up. Relieved.

I clean myself up and roll the jeans and knickers into a ball, carry them into my bedroom and stuff them into my rucksack. In the morning I'll throw them into the bin at the end of the road and work out an excuse.

I put on my shellsuit and go downstairs. My huge leap towards womanhood personifies itself in a roly-poly into the centre of the living room.

'Sit quietly, Renée. Your nana is watching her programme,' Pop snaps.

I crawl up onto the sofa. It's quite hard to sit quietly in a shellsuit.

Flo

As soon as I meet Sally outside Boots I know I am in for a horrible Saturday. She is so angry with me for sitting in the library with Renée, but at the same time so full of herself because I chose to go with her.

'I bet Renée can't afford to go shopping,' she says in her usual snarky tone.

'Well, her family aren't rich like yours.'

'Do you think she is trendy? I don't. Her clothes are so nondescript.'

'She is just totally unaffected by fashion. I think that's quite cool,' I say, determined not to encourage her.

'There is nothing cool about Renée Sargent. And stop going on about her, will you? I thought today was supposed to be about me,' she says, storming off.

'Every day is about you, Sally,' I say under my breath as she marches into Pandora and starts scraping the clothes along the rails. I sit on the sofa outside the changing rooms and hope this goes quickly.

With an arm full of clothes, she goes into the changing room and tears the curtain across so hard that it nearly falls down. She pokes her head out and hisses, 'You should be grateful you have me. I'm the reason you have a life at all. I'll try these on, then you can pass those in one by

187

one and I'll try them on while you put these ones back. I think Phil will prefer the short dresses.'

'Who is Phil?' I ask, deliberately trying to annoy her.

'I TOLD YOU, he works with my dad. He's twenty-seven. We are going out.'

'You're going out with a twenty-seven-year-old? How does your dad feel about that?' I am genuinely interested to know how that is working out.

'He doesn't know, but he'll be fine once he realises it's serious.'

'Have you . . .' I buckle at the thought of talking about sex with Sally. It feels far too unnatural to have a conversation like that with her. Luckily she knows what I mean.

'No, not yet. But he wants to, I can tell. But you wouldn't understand because you'll probably be a virgin forever.' She cackles like a witch. 'Hold this.' She throws another top over my arm and scrapes the curtain back across. I stand staring at it. My arm is weighted down by the huge pile of clothing she's hung over it. A moment of clarity comes over me. This isn't what friendship is about, I know that now.

'Sally?' I say boldly.

She tuts. I hear a zip go up and a clear note of disappointment in her next tut, this one not aimed at me.

'Sally?' I say again.

The zip goes back down and I see the dress drop to her feet under the curtain. She still doesn't acknowledge me.

'SALLY?' I rip open the curtain. She is facing away from me, bending down to pick up the dress, her bony

188

bum up in the air for all the shop to see. She spins around, her arms covering her boobs, her face a vision of pure horror.

'WHAT ARE YOU DOING? CLOSE THAT NOW!' she screeches.

I push the curtain open even further, enjoying the power I feel for once.

'Sally, for ten years I have let you treat me like some shit on the bottom of your shoe. You boss me around, put me down, embarrass me all the time. I've had enough. I'm not the pathetic idiot you think I am, and you, you are such a bitch.'

I drop the clothes on the floor and turn to leave. Her face is frozen from the shock of my outburst. I feel a thousand feet tall.

'Flo, FLO! Come back here, Flo! Don't you walk away from me!'

I turn back to her. She looks ridiculous. My voice remains perfectly calm.

'Our friendship is over, Sally. I don't need to be treated like this any more. My other friends are *nice* to me.'

'Other friends? Like you have any other friends. Oh wait, you mean Renée Sargent? Ha, she will ditch you the minute something better comes along. At least I've stuck by you, which isn't easy sometimes, because you are so boring. Flo, if you walk away from me now you will always regret it. You're nothing without me.'

'No, *you* are nothing without me.' I realise I'm shaking, but I keep going. 'The only reason you've stuck by me is because I've stuck by you and without me YOU have no one else. And Sally?'

'WHAT?'

'You have a skid mark.'

I leave the shop to the sound of her wailing and walk through town feeling so proud of myself that I could scream. I want to run up to strangers and tell them what I just did. This has to be one of the best moments of my life. The deed is done – Renée and I are free to be friends. Sally is officially out of the picture. I can't wait to tell Renée.

Renée

Saturdays are usually so boring at home, but today is different. I want to do nothing but lie on my bed and think about Julian. Time is flying by, the hours lost just thinking about him and that night in the car. I want more of it. I keep thinking about how much more confident I will be next time, how sexy I will act, how much I could turn him on if he only knew the real me. He doesn't know how funny I am yet either. I will make him laugh next time, then I'll give him a perfect blow job and I will definitely go on top.

The doorbell rings.

Renée,' calls Pop. 'Someone is here for you.'

I jump up in a split second. Shit shit shit, what if it's

him? I'm wearing my shellsuit. I try to get out of it, hopping on one foot. The left leg gets stuck and I fall backwards onto the floor. My bedroom door opens slowly.

'Renée?' Flo's head peers in and she sees me lying there – red-faced in a panic with my shellsuit around my ankles. 'Is that a shellsuit?' she asks, confused.

'I just found it in my wardrobe. I put it on for a laugh.' I pull up the shellsuit and sit on my bed. I feel like such a twat. 'What are you doing here?'

She comes further into my bedroom and looks around. 'I like your room,' she says. I know she is lying. It's horrible. Pop won't let us put up posters, and the wallpaper is old. I've never had a friend come into it before, and suddenly I feel very uncomfortable for a whole load of other reasons than I already do. Can she tell Mum died almost exactly where I am sitting?

'What are you doing here?' I ask again.

She sits down next to me on the bed. She looks happy with herself.

'I told Sally. I told Sally where to go and how horrible she is, and I left her in a changing room with no clothes on and it feels totally amazing. It's the best thing I've ever done.'

'Oh, right. That's great. Good for you,' I say, almost completely without emotion. I know I am being mean but can't help it.

'I thought it was what you wanted? We don't have to sneak around any more.'

'Great. Sneaking around, yeah that was bad, wasn't it?'

191

I can't even look at Flo. It must have taken every shred of confidence she had to stand up to Sally, but I can't look at her without imagining myself with Julian in his car and how she would feel if she knew.

'Renée, we are going for a drive,' shouts Pop up the stairs.

'What is it about old people and going for drives?' I say, laughing. Flo looks more confused. I know I should say something about Sally.

'Wait there, Pop. I'll come with you,' I shout, as I frantically pull on my trainers.

'You are going to go with your grandparents for a drive?' Flo asks. 'In a shellsuit? Don't you want to go out and celebrate the fact that we can be best friends in public now?'

'I need chewing gum,' is all I can think of to say as I usher her out of the house and climb into the back of Pop's car. As we drive away I watch Flo standing at the end of our driveway looking absolutely gutted. I feel like the biggest bitch ever.

As Pop pulls into a petrol station Nana is muttering something about ice creams, but I've gone back to thinking about Julian. Eventually he and I will tell Flo what happened, and all of this will be fine. She will understand that we couldn't help ourselves. She will be my best friend and he will be my boyfriend and all this tension will have gone. I really do hate lying to her, but I can't tell her yet. It's too soon.

'Here,' says Pop, handing me a small bundle of notes. 'Go and pay for the fuel and buy Nana a Cornetto. You can have one too.'

I get out of the car, my head still a million miles away from reality. As I walk across the forecourt and up to the shop I see him, bending over under the bonnet of a car, a spanner in his hand. I'd recognise him from any angle anywhere in the world, no matter what he was wearing. What are the chances of me just stumbling across him at work? I didn't even know which garage he worked at. I have no choice but to embrace this as a sign that we are meant to be together. This is no coincidence, this is the universe helping me out.

I walk over. This is my chance to show him who I really am. Cool, confident, grown-up, completely together.

'Hi, Julian,' I say, trying to be casual.

He turns around. He has a piece of something rubbery in between his teeth. He spits it out and it lands on the floor.

'Is that a shellsuit?' he asks. He looks repulsed.

SHIT, shit, shit, shit. In the shock of seeing him I forgot I was wearing it. I scramble around in my brain for something to tell him.

'It's fancy dress. I'm on my way to a party. I'm a Chuckle Brother,' I say, blushing.

'A fancy dress party? At two in the afternoon?' He doesn't look convinced.

'It's my little sister's party,' I say, hoping he doesn't already know that my 'little sister' is actually thirteen.

'Right, well, off you go then.' He turns back to the car and carries on fixing it.

Confident. Come on, Renée. Be confident.

'Do you want an ice cream?' I ask, instantly regretting it.

He laughs. But the wrong kind of laugh. He is laughing at me. He turns back to face me.

'No, I don't want an ice cream, because I am a grown-up. And what are you turning up to my work for? Are you a stalker or something?'

I feel so stupid. This all looks so deliberate.

'No,' I say. 'No, I didn't just turn up. We were out for a drive and we just stopped for ice cream. I didn't know you were here.'

He looks over at Nana and Pop, who have just noticed that I haven't gone into the shop yet. 'Sure you didn't. Anyway, you'd better hurry up. Your friends are waiting for you.' He turns back to the car.

I stand watching him for a few seconds but even I, in my delirious loved-up state, know when I am not wanted. I go inside and buy Nana her ice cream. I have completely lost my appetite.

9
Dribbles Down the Side of a Pan

Renée

'Renée, wake up. Wake up.' Nana is prodding me.

'What time is it?'

'It's 7 a.m. There's someone on the phone for you. It sounds important. Come on, up you get, but don't wake your sister.' Nana gives me a little shake.

Who is calling me at 7 a.m? I don't think I have ever had a phone call at 7 a.m. I put on my dressing gown and rush down to the kitchen.

'Hello?'

'Hey, it's Flo.'

My throat closes up. Does she know?

'Are you sitting comfortably?'

I brace myself for the biggest character assassination of

195

my life. I feel evil, pure evil. I should have told her about me and Julian myself.

'Yes.'

'Good. OK, Abi, ONE, TWO, THREE . . . Happy birthday to you, happy birthday to you, happy birthday to Renée, happy birthday to youuuuuuuuu. We wanted to be the first ones to say happy birthday. Sweet sixteen, and all that.' She speaks quietly into the receiver. 'You are old enough to do it now! WOO HOOO!'

'Thanks,' I say, relieved. Of course, it's the 9th of March. My birthday. 'Wow, it's so early. I thought something terrible had happened.'

'Nope. Life is good, Renée. It's nothing terrible at all. Go get ready and get to school early. I have pressies!' Flo says, full of excitement.

I hang up. Something tells me my relief won't last forever.

'Was it about some homework?' asks Nana as she comes into the kitchen. She walks straight past me and over to the sink, no Happy Birthday, no nothing.

'No, Nana, my friend didn't call me at 7 a.m. about homework.'

'Well, what a funny time to call for a chat. I hope she doesn't make a habit of it.'

I want to tell her, 'Nana, it's my birthday,' but she will be so upset with herself for forgetting. I don't want to embarrass her.

'I'm going in early today. We have a computer project on so I'm going to meet with my group before school starts.'

'Computers?' says Pop as he comes into the kitchen. 'What a waste of time. They should be teaching you trade skills rather than wasting time on those machines. Don't wake your sister up as you get dressed. She needs her sleep.'

'I won't.'

I walk past the calendar on the kitchen wall. It's still on December. Life in our house is officially not moving forward.

'SURRPPPRRRIIISEEEE!'

When I walk into our form room Flo, Margaret, Nancy, Bethan and Charlotte are all wearing their green science smocks and waving hockey sticks at me.

'What are you all wearing?' I ask.

'Flo only reminded me it was your birthday last night so we didn't have time to sort fancy dress out. Hockey sticks and smocks is the best we could do,' explains Margaret. 'But look what we got for lunchtime.'

She empties two plastic bags full of crisps and cakes onto the floor. 'For a table party. We have enough food to feed everyone in the school and it's all ours!'

Table parties are a tradition at Tudor Falls. Whenever someone has a birthday during term time everyone at their table brings in as many cakes and sandwiches and crisps as they can. We are even allowed party poppers and hats. For Tudor Falls this really is as wild as it gets.

The dining room is divided into tables of six. At the beginning of every year you choose who you want on your

197

table and that is the way it stays. Margaret, Charlotte, Bethan, Nancy and I always have a spare place at our table because no one else wants to sit with us in case they get into trouble for being too noisy, but a couple of weeks ago Flo asked the teachers if she could move and join us. 'It's about you and me now,' she said as she opened her lunch box. My stomach flipped. I knew I should have taken her outside and told her there and then.

I pick up a packet of Mr Kipling Apple Slices and help myself.

'Don't eat it all now. We won't have any left for lunchtime,' begs Margaret, like our lunch is the only meal we will ever eat again.

'Get lost, it's my birthday. I'm going to eat all day,' I say.

We all sit on the floor at the back of the classroom and eat cake. Flo gives me some presents all wrapped individually in pink and green paper. There's a scrunchie, a pencil case with 'I must, I must, I must improve my maths' on it, and a rubber in the shape of some fish and chips. I find it hard to look her in the eye as I thank her. I wish she hadn't done this. I find myself wondering if she has told Julian it's my birthday, and if he is thinking about me at all. It's been weeks since that day at the garage. I haven't dared go back to their house in case he thinks I am stalking him, but not seeing him is making me crazy. I am obsessed with him and tired of making excuses to Flo about why I am being so distant with her. She thinks

I am stressed about Pop, and the exams, but I'm not. I'm just hopelessly in love with her brother.

At break time I grab Margaret and try to get out of school and down the lane before anyone else sees us. 'Come on, let's go smoke,' I say, as I drag her by the arm.

'Renée, wait!' calls Flo after us. 'Wait for me.'

I power forward as if I haven't heard her. Margaret resists me. 'Renée, stop. Flo wants you. Renée, stop pulling me!'

'Could you not hear me?' asks Flo as she catches up. 'I was calling you. I've barely seen you since I told Sally where to go. She really has backed off. It's good, isn't it?'

'Sorry. I just really need a fag,' I say, looking at the ground.

'Can I come with you?' she asks.

'But you don't smoke.'

'I know, but . . .'

I take a deep breath. 'Flo, you don't have to follow me everywhere, you know? It's OK for us to be apart for like, five minutes.'

The world seems to stop moving for a few seconds.

'OK, fine. I'll wait here,' she says, eventually.

'Good.'

She turns slowly and walks back into school. I watch her, hating myself.

'What did you do that for?' asks Margaret.

I gather myself and keep walking. 'She can be a bit too needy sometimes, that's all.'

I want the ground to swallow me up.

At lunchtime, the atmosphere is tense.

'OK, ladies, stand up, please. Let's say grace.' It's Miss Anthony's day on lunch duty. When everyone has drawn to a silent pause Margaret does her favourite trick of scraping her chair backwards across the shiny floor, making a screeching sound so piercing that everyone puts their hands to their ears.

'WHEN you are ready, ladies! For what we are about to receive . . .' continues Miss Anthony.

We all join in, then in unison scrape our chairs as we sit down.

'Hey,' says Nancy in a loud whisper. We all lean in. 'I heard that Becca Stephens lost her virginity at the weekend.'

A brilliant start to the lunchtime conversation, and the perfect ice breaker.

'Yeah, I heard that too,' adds Charlotte. 'To some guy in the year above us at the boys' school. She isn't even sixteen yet.'

'Loads of people have done it before they are sixteen, stupid,' says Nancy.

'You haven't,' says Margaret in her usual matter-of-fact style.

'Yeah, well, none of us have!' says Bethan.

Nancy's defensiveness is now standard when girls in Year 11 discuss their virginity. I'm not sure when this

200

happened, but suddenly being called a virgin is an insult.

'I guess it isn't when you lose it, it's who you lose it to that matters,' says Flo. All the girls nod in agreement. I sit back and stuff as much cake into my mouth as possible. I don't want to say anything that might later be used in evidence against me.

As we plough through our feast a loud screech comes from the other side of the dining room, then the sound of a chair falling over, and then a loud scream for help. I look up and see a crowd gathering and Miss Anthony calling to the caretaker, 'Ambulance, call an ambulance!'

'Renée, Renée! Quick, get over here!' a girl from the year below us is calling me. I'm not sure what I am expected to do in an emergency. I lied about passing my St John's Ambulance First Aid course last year as it seemed like such a waste of a Saturday morning.

'Quick, Renée! QUICK!' says the girl.

The crowd parts to let me through. What's going on? There is mayhem all of a sudden. And then I see her – my sister, lying in the arms of one of her classmates. Her head flopped right back, her long thin body limp, her eyes and her mouth half open.

'NELL!'

I take her into my arms and shake her. She is so bony she could rattle.

'NELL!'

'OK, girls, give them some space. The ambulance is on its way,' says Miss Anthony.

Flo is behind me, her hands holding onto my shoulders.

I twist awkwardly until she lets go, and feel her hurt as she backs away from me.

Nell, I think. *Just focus on Nell.*

At the hospital I'm told to wait in the hall. 'We will come and tell you when you can come in and see your sister,' says a nurse.

'Will she be OK?' I ask, frightened.

'She is very weak, but it's nothing some fluids can't treat for now. Your sister is going to need a lot of help to get well again though; a lot of help,' says the nurse.

I watch her scuttle back down the corridor, her big bottom moving as two halves. I grip my knees with my hands and wait.

'Renée!' The double doors open slowly and Nana and Pop come towards me. I am shocked by how they look. When did they get so old? Nana used to be tall and slim, now she is little and round, her body moving differently. She looks in pain. And Pop, he was tall and handsome but now he is stooped over and his face looks like it's melting. How had I not noticed this change?

'Where is she? Nurse, we are here to see Nell Sargent,' says Nana.

'We can't go in yet, Pop,' I tell him. 'They say she will be OK after some fluids but that we have to wait here until she is ready to see us.'

Pop sits robotically on a bench, Nana next to him. I sit opposite them, my mind still battered by how old they look.

'What happened? Did she fall?' Nana asks.

'She fainted.'

'Fainted? It's so hot in that school. Haven't I always said it is too hot in that school?' grumbles Pop.

'She didn't faint because it was hot, Derek,' Nana says firmly.

'I'll write to that caretaker again. He should know better than to keep the school so hot.'

We all stand up when a doctor walks over to us.

'Mr and Mrs Fletcher? Hello, I'm Dr Brehaut. Nell is ready to see you now.'

We follow Dr Brehaut down the hall. She opens the door to Nell's room and I go straight over to where she is lying.

'Nell, I'm so glad you are OK,' I say frantically. 'You fainted and your eyes were rolling. I thought you . . .'

She has a hospital gown on and a drip in the back of her hand. She is awake and the relief I feel when I see her makes me start crying, which is embarrassing for me and clearly awkward for everyone else.

'Sorry to drag you away from the party of the century. I could hear that Margaret Cooper weirdo singing Happy Birthday to you from my table. She is so loud,' Nell says, still managing to be sarcastic even in her state.

'Renée, your birthday?' says Nana as she puts her hands to her face.

'Don't worry, Nana, it's OK.'

'No, no, it's not OK.' She lowers her voice and looks really sad. 'I'm sorry.'

'Now, now. Let's not overblow this. Your nana and I are very sorry we forgot your birthday, Renée,' says Pop, rubbing his forehead.

'It's fine, honestly,' I say. 'I think we should all just focus on Nell. My birthday isn't important.'

Nana takes Nell's hand in hers. She looks guilty. 'How are you feeling, darling? I know you have been unwell.'

Nell doesn't offer Nana any words of reassurance. I think she's enjoying the impact she is having on us all.

'Mr and Mrs Fletcher, can I ask you to step outside with me for a moment?' says Dr Brehaut.

They all leave the room and stand just outside. I can see them through the window in the door. Dr Brehaut looks serious, and as she talks to them they both drop their heads at exactly the same moment. Nana starts to cry.

Nell and I sit awkwardly together.

'Hopefully now they'll understand that they can't keep me away from my dad.'

'*Now?*'

'Now that it's come to this,' she says, gesturing towards the drip in her hand.

'Nell, you could have died.'

'I know. But I didn't. So they should listen to me now. They can't keep me away from my own dad any more. It isn't fair.'

I think back to the time I tried to speak to Nana, when I'd been so determined to sort all of this out but didn't see it through. I'd let Pop intimidate me and I let the moment pass. I could have stopped this happening but instead I let it carry on and now my little sister is committing a long slow suicide to try and make them notice how much she is hurting. Nell was right, this is all my fault. Everything is.

When Nana and Pop come in again, Pop stands at the back of the room while Nana goes over to Nell.

'We will help you get through this, Nell. As a family. We can help you. Just tell us what we need to do. What do you need?' Nana says, crying.

'Dad, Nana. I need my dad,' says Nell.

Pop leaves the room, making sure the door slams shut behind him. But she is right – this time he has to listen.

Later that night, as I face the first night alone in our bedroom since Mum died in it, I wonder how it would be if Nell was to go and live with Dad. What would happen to me? Terrible as my relationship with her is, I don't want to sleep in this room on my own.

I don't feel in control of anything. It's all such a mess. I think back to what Miss Anthony suggested, to write a letter to the person who is hurting me the most. I never have to give it to them; it's just for me. I have to clear up this mess. This is where it starts. I begin to write.

Dear Julian . . .

Flo

I think Renée has gone off me and it's horrible. I don't know what I've done wrong but I've obviously really annoyed her. Did I go on about my dad too much? Was I too boring? Did I say something mean? I've read through every note she ever wrote to me and I don't see anything that has been said that should make her change her mind about being my friend, but it's so obvious she doesn't want to be around me and I feel like such a fool. Now I've dumped Sally and Renée has dumped me, I am left totally friendless. I feel so unhappy, my tummy is in knots, and the last thing I want is to go into town with my mother to buy some short-sleeved school shirts.

'You don't have to come with me. If you give me the money I can just buy the shirts myself,' I say as she storms into the uniform shop.

'And let you loose with my money?' my mum says, as if she has reason to think I am untrustworthy.

'I've never used your money for anything other than what you've told me to use it for,' I say.

'That's because I would never give you the chance. Not like that father of yours, throwing cash at you like it grows on trees. Like that school he put you in, leaving me behind to pay the ridiculous fees.'

'Well, Mother, I am very grateful to you for giving me the chance to have an education.'

'You're not grateful. Why can't you be more like her? At least she has a job.' My mum points at the rotund girl behind the counter who is wearing elasticated jeans, an apron, and a name badge that says 'Jenny'.

Jenny has worked in Hemans – the uniform shop – for as long as I can remember. Every year I've watched her large bottom disappear up a ladder to get the uniform in my size down from the top shelf, and every year she looks the same – around seventeen years old and hauntingly miserable. Dad and I always presumed that she is part of the family who own the shop, because she is as much a part of it as the shelves that fill it.

'You wish I was more like Jenny?' I ask sarcastically.

'At least she pays her way.'

How Mum thinks I could have a job, as well as study and look after Abi, is beyond me. I bite my tongue and ask Jenny to get me some shirts.

'The size 40 is best. I like them a bit loose,' I say. I'm two sizes bigger than last year, not because I am fat, but because my boobs are huge. I hand three shirts to Jenny at the till, and she starts to put them in a bag. Mum gets some cash out of her purse and hands it to Jenny.

'Get the change and be quick. I'll wait outside,' she snaps as she leaves.

Jenny and I stand quietly as she opens the till and works out the change.

'There you go, £5.01,' she says, handing me the money.

'Thanks.' I go to leave.

'Flo? Your name is Flo, isn't it?'

I look at the money in my hand. Has she miscalculated the change? It doesn't look like it.

'I've worked in here every Saturday since I was twelve and as soon as I turned sixteen my mum made me leave school and go full time,' she tells me. 'You're lucky you get to go to school, and have lots of friends. I don't have any friends. I'd love your life.'

No one has ever told me they would love my life before.

'It's not all that,' I say to her. 'I bet there are loads of things about your life that I would be jealous of.'

I wait for her to answer me, but she doesn't say anything.

'FLO, hurry up!' Mum screeches as she swoops back in and grabs the fiver out of my hand.

I turn back to Jenny. I never thought about her feelings before. It's easy to just take people for what they seem, and not think about what life is actually like for them. It makes me think about Renée, and how she has been behaving towards me. It's easy to presume she is all right because of how confident she is, but her sister collapsed because she is so ill, things at home are bad, and Renée obviously isn't coping.

It hits me like a shock that I need to be a better friend to Renée. I've been so hurt by how distant she has been from me lately, but I have to stand by her. If she wants to push me away or use me as a punch bag then fine, but I'll still be there for her when she feels better. It's the least I can do after she pretty much saved me when Dad died.

208

Renée

It's hard to concentrate at school at the best of times, let alone when your sister is in hospital being force-fed calories through a tube, your family is as functional as a broken toilet, you're treating your best friend like shit because you feel so guilty and the boy you love thinks you are a stalker who wears shellsuits. Pop had a massive go at me as I left for school this morning. He was going on and on about how I fill Nell's head with rubbish and how I should be a better example to her. I don't know what to say to him when he gets like that with me. Even Nana doesn't try to stop him. He locks on to something and doesn't let go and I am sick of how that something always seems to be me. I'm over being the baddy all the time, and nothing good that I do ever getting noticed. GCSEs are the last thing on my mind.

I sit in science class slumped on my stool like I have fallen out of the sky and broken my spine. To top it off I have been moved permanently to the front bench after the incident with the vegetarians so I can't even gaze out of the window without being told off. For once in my life I want to be completely unnoticed. I have problems, real problems. Loads of them. Life is shit.

A paper aeroplane hits me on the back of the head. It hurts.

I have worked out that if you put blue tac in the nose then the notes fly further. Flo x

209

What is she talking about? I ignore her note. Another one hits me.

Renée, are you OK? I know you've been really upset lately. I don't mind you taking things out on me a bit but I just wanted to let you know that I am here for you if you need me. You have been the best friend in the world to me, and I want to be the same to you. If you want to talk, I'm here. You don't deserve all the stuff that's going on in your life and I am on your side. Flo x

Why is everyone else allowed a bad day except me? I spend my life giving people space, letting them thump around all angry and stressed while I just leave them to it and let them deal with their own shit. Why is it that when I have a bad day no one will leave me alone and let me just be pissed off on my own? If I dare give even the smallest hint that I'm an emotionally volatile person I get told off, called moody, selfish or to pull myself together. I can't be happy all the time!

I ignore her letter again. I will talk to her soon and tell her everything, but right now I have enough on my plate. Mrs Suiter picks up a pile of exam papers and starts to make her way around the class.

'Well done, Margaret. Very good,' she says as she lays her exam paper in front of her.

'Wow, 73%!' Margaret looks very pleased with herself, as does Charlotte.

'75%, YES!'

And Flo: '85%. I can't believe it.'

Then Mrs Suiter gives me mine.

'See me after class, please, Renée.'

23%. Oh, bloody hell!

When the bell rings, I stay put.

As Flo walks past me she puts her hand on my shoulder. I shake it off. I don't even realise I do it until she looks back at me with the most pitiful eyes I've ever seen.

'This is unacceptable, Renée. Did you do any revision at all?' Mrs Suiter says sternly.

'Sorry, Mrs Suiter. Things have been really tough at home recently and I'm finding it really hard to concentrate,' I say, looking notably upset.

She looks at me with the 'don't give me that' expression that I usually get from teachers when I make up excuses for not doing well at school, but then her face changes and she gives me a much more sympathetic look.

'Yes, well, we are all hoping that Nell gets better soon,' she says gently.

I sit waiting for my order mark, but it never comes. Instead she stares me in the eye in her usual intense way.

'Life is tough sometimes, but without good exam results it will only get tougher. You must try to focus, no matter what is going on at home.'

'I know, Mrs Suiter, I will try harder. I'm just finding everything really hard and . . .' Tears start pelting down my face. It's uncontrollable. Damn it, I hate crying in front of teachers. Mrs Suiter also obviously feels as uncomfortable and stares at me even more intensely.

211

'Now now, Renée. It's just a mock exam. There is plenty of time to do some revision for your GCSEs.'

'It's not just my exams,' I say, giving into the tears.

'Maybe you should pop home? I'll tell Miss Anthony you felt a bit sick and that I excused you. Then you can go home and see your family. Will that help?'

I think for a moment about seeing my family and wonder what a life where the thought of them didn't make me want to bolt would feel like, but I can't imagine it. I miss Flo so much. What have I done? She was the best friend I ever had and now I have made our friendship impossible because being with her makes me feel awful and two-faced.

I feel a pang of regret for pushing Carla and Gem away. When I was friends with them at least life was simple. They don't have the brain capacity, or emotional intelligence, or whatever it is, to worry about life. If we were still friends I could have told them about Julian. They'd have told me I am funny and that he is mean, and they'd have hugged me until I didn't care about him any more, but as it stands I care about him more than anything else. More than Nell, more than Nana and Pop, my GCSEs, anything. I never thought I would be so bothered about my virginity, but having lost it I wish I still had it. I held off for all that time with Lawrence because I didn't want the entire experience to leave me feeling like shit and here I am, feeling like total shit. I keep going over and over it in my head – and then I think of the blood. That huge red stain surrounding my crotch. Why would he ever want

212

to have sex with me again now? Everything about it makes me want to crawl into a hole and die.

'Yes please, I'll go home and see my family,' I say to Mrs Suiter.

I am excused. I go straight to the hospital.

As I walk up the corridor towards Nell's room I'm not sure if I will go in or not. I can't possibly go home at eleven thirty as Pop would never believe that I have been excused from school. I think I might just look through the glass, check Nell is OK, then sit in the corridor and read magazines until lunchtime. Then, maybe I'll brave going home and tell Pop I have a headache, and then I'll get into bed and cry until I have to go to school again tomorrow. I expect this will be my life forever.

As I approach Nell's room the door is open. I hear voices, female voices. Nell is talking to a woman. A young woman, not Nana. The tone is affectionate – I can tell it isn't a nurse. Then I recognise the voice. It goes through me like honey in my veins. It's unmistakable. It's my mother's voice.

I stand listening. Every part of me vibrating at a million miles per hour.

'I love you very much, Nell, and I've missed you. We'll all get through this together.'

It's her. That dream I had, the one where she had gone into hiding because the police are after her, it was true. My mum is back. Everything is going to change.

My feet start to run and I burst into Nell's room with eyes so wide I can't see straight.

'MUM.' It comes out of me so loud that Nell gasps for breath at the shock of it.

'Renée, what the . . .?'

The three of us are still. I stand staring at my mother, my eyes slowly adjusting, my breath steadying to a pace that I can cope with. Her face comes into focus.

'Renée.'

She walks towards me. Her face looks all wrong. What is wrong with her face? It is wrong, why is it wrong? I start to cry.

'Renée, Renée. It's me. Aunty Jo.'

Three hard blinks later and the reality is almost as good as the dream. Aunty Jo, Mum's sister, the second most perfect person I have ever met. I throw myself around her, I can't get close enough. There it is, the smell of Chanel No. 5, leather and cigarettes. The best smell in the world. She feels like her, smells like her and sounds like her. For the few minutes that I stand with every part of me as close to her as I can get it, I forget about everyone else.

'It's OK, darling, I'm back now. I'm not going anywhere this time.'

She strokes my hair. When no one has stroked your hair in five years it feels like they are kissing you right on the heart.

'How did you know to come?' I ask, my face squashed against her.

'Nana called me. It's going to be OK. We will work this all out.'

* * *

214

Aunty Jo kept me out of school for the next week. Nell came home from hospital and even though she is still so thin and ill, she sits with us at dinner and we all talk. The conversation is awkward and feels strange for everybody, but at least it's happening. Pop hasn't been cutting me down as much over the past few days. I imagine he probably wants to, but maybe being the only man around four women makes him feel a little outnumbered.

One night at dinner I can tell something is brewing. Aunty Jo is about to tell us something serious.

'Nell, Renée, there is something we need to tell you,' she says when we have all finished our homemade chicken in white wine sauce. I feel a rush of fear as I prepare for her to tell us she is leaving again.

'I have spoken to your father,' Aunty Jo says gently.

Nell stands to attention. Part excited, part ready to attack.

'We spoke for a long time and, Nell, he and I think that it would be a good idea for you to go and stay with him,' Aunty Jo says, occasionally glancing at Pop as if to control him.

Nell's face changes shape. Her sunken skin plumps up and everything moves upwards as she smiles like I haven't seen her smile for years.

'Really?' she says, wide-eyed.

'Yes. Dr Brehaut says she is happy for you to go, but you will have to continue to see a doctor there. If all goes well *then* maybe you can look into the local schools in Spain. If your father and you feel that the right thing would be for you to stay,' Aunty Jo says, nodding at Pop to encourage him to say something,

I look at Pop. He keeps his eyes on his plate. A reluctant nod expresses his agreement. 'It is only right that you should be with your father,' he says like he's being squeezed. 'If it doesn't work out, you can always come back.'

'It will work out,' says Nell with such conviction I know she will never live with us again. She scoops some chicken onto her fork and confidently eats it. She has what she wanted.

In the midst of everyone's moment I find myself unable to feel happy. 'What about me?' I ask, bracing myself for a barrage of comments about how I always think about myself.

'You're going to live with me,' says Aunty Jo. 'I'm moving back to Guernsey permanently.'

I look at Nana. Her eyes are full of tears but she is smiling. Pop nods as he continues to stare at his plate.

'Really? With you? When?' I ask, so happy I could scream but too aware of Nana's feelings to dare.

'As soon as I find us a house,' Aunty Jo continues. 'I'm looking at some over the next few days. Seeing as I have persuaded school to excuse you for a week, why don't you come with me? It will be your home, after all. You have to like it.'

I nod so enthusiastically that I burp. Everyone laughs.

Later on I am sitting in my room with the door open reading *Smash Hits* when I hear someone coming up the stairs. I quickly throw the magazine on the floor, open my science textbook and sit up straight. Pop walks past my room and goes into the bathroom. I don't look up. A few moments later he comes out and just after he passes my door he stops. I feel nervous. He turns back and comes into my room. He has not been in here with me since the moment he pulled me away from Mum, minutes before she died.

The memory of it floods back like it was yesterday, and when I look at him I know he is thinking the same thing. For a moment we look at each other as if that is enough to express how we are feeling, but it isn't. I jump off my bed and run into his open arms.

'You are just like her,' he says as he sobs into my hair. 'You are just like her.'

The next few days of house hunting are so much fun. In between viewings Aunty Jo and I go to nice cafes, and she even takes me into town to buy some new clothes. I feel like my head is gradually getting together.

'Where will you work now you are back?' I ask, as we sift through the rails in Pandora.

'I'll work it out. The only good thing that came out of the last few years is a nice divorce settlement. I'll be OK for a bit.'

'Why did you leave Uncle Andrew?' I ask, cautiously.

'Let's just say I finally admitted to myself that he didn't love me as much as he should have done.'

'What do you mean, finally? You mean you always knew?'

'Yup. Ever since I met him I had to fight for his attention, prove to him that I was worthy of him. It shouldn't be like that. People either love you, or they don't. You can't force it on someone. I knew as I walked down the aisle towards him that he would never love me like I loved him. If I had been honest with myself about that back then, then the last five years of my life would have been very different. But hey, you live and learn, right?' Aunty Jo says with a shrug.

'Right,' I say.

And there it is. My biggest remaining problem ironed out, giving me the moment of clarity that I have been waiting for. Julian will never want me – he made that perfectly clear at the garage. I either lose my best friend trying to make him, or I concentrate on the person who I care about the most. I have to tell Flo the truth and save our friendship. It's the most important thing. Julian isn't worth losing Flo over. I just hope I'm not too late.

10

The Letter of
Mass Destruction

Flo

As I walk to school I wonder if today will be the day that Renée comes back. It's only been a week but Tudor Falls feels empty without her. Renée is the one who brings everyone together. Without her people just get on with school. I've missed her so much.

When I walk into the classroom Sally is already at her desk.

'Oh, morning, Flo. How are you?' she asks cheerily.

What's she playing at? She is being nice. I don't like it.

I open my desk. She has put a Wagon Wheel in it.

'I know they're your favourite. I have a multipack in my bag. You can have one every day this week if you like.'

What? No lecture about how chocolate makes me spotty? What is going on?

She smiles at me. A freakishly wide smile showing no teeth. She is scaring me.

'Sally, why are you being like this?' I ask suspiciously.

'What? Can't I give my best friend some chocolate?'

'You are not my . . .' I think better of carrying on. I can't be bothered to go through it again. The unfortunate rule that we are not allowed to change seats in our form room means that I have to be next to her for twenty minutes every morning during registration. After that I can avoid her all day. I take a deep breath and sit tight. I can cope with her for twenty minutes, just. Miss Anthony comes in.

'Good morning, everybody. Ah, and good morning, Renée. Welcome back.'

I turn around. Renée is standing at her desk. She looks happier. I smile and will the next twenty minutes to go really quickly so I can tell her how much I've missed her. As I gather my books for the morning's classes, a note hits me on the head. Sally sees it but ignores it. Finally we have progress.

I've missed you. We need to talk. Can we meet after school? R x

I reply immediately.

I missed you tooooooo! I've been so worried ab

A gasp from the back of the room makes me stop writing and look up. Miss Anthony has pulled down the blackboard and on it, in large chalky letters, I see the words 'Dear Julian'. My eyes fixed on the board, I continue to read.

Dear Julian,
The night I met you I'd found Flo passed out at Gem's house about to have her period all over the floor. I had to stuff loo roll into her pants and then pretty much carry her home. It was gross, but when I saw you I didn't mind any more. I wouldn't have met you if she hadn't got so wasted.

Then that time in the kitchen when you kissed me, and you touched me the way that you did, I think that's when I fell in love with you. I kept making excuses to come to your house after that.

And then that night when I lied to Flo about feeling ill and we had sex in your car, that was one of the worst and best nights of my life. But I worry that I wasn't good enough, that I didn't do it right. I worry about all the blood. My white jeans were stained so badly I had to throw them away. I know that might have put you off, but please give me another chance. Maybe Flo never needs to know?

'OH MY GOD! My jeans!!' screeches Gem from the back of the class. 'My mum is going to flip out!'

I feel like a piano is stuck in my throat.

'Is this a joke?' I say, standing up and rising above Sally, who is sitting at her desk. I'll make her tell me this isn't

221

true if is the last thing I do. She hands me a piece of paper. My eyes go straight to the end.

I know you will think I'm too young to say this, but I think I love you.
Renée

I'd recognise Renée's writing anywhere. I stare at the letter. I have to remind myself to breathe.

'OK, ladies, let's all keep calm. Sally, did you make this up?' asks Miss Anthony.

All eyes turn to Sally. Every single person in the room is expecting her to admit to making this up. Everyone knows she is capable of it.

'No, no, she didn't,' I eventually say, turning to Renée. 'I have the letter here in my hand. It's true. Renée wrote this.'

I watch Renée fall into her seat and drop her head into her hands.

'I don't feel very well, Miss Anthony,' I say like a zombie. 'Can I go home?'

Miss Anthony thinks for a few seconds then excuses me. I bolt for the door and run all the way home, where I shut myself in my bedroom and pull the duvet over my head. I never want to go back to school, ever ever again.

Renée

I wait outside the toilet cubicle.

'Come out, Sally. The least you can do is face me after what you just did to Flo.'

The door flies open.

'What *I* did to Flo? Um . . . I think you'll find you did that all yourself,' she says, strutting past me.

She goes over to the sinks and stares at her spiteful face in the mirror.

'How did you get the letter?' I ask, trying to keep my cool. 'It was in my bedroom, how did you get it?'

'You'll never know,' she says smugly.

'Tell me, Sally, how did you get it?' I push, really trying to stay calm.

She laughs. An evil laugh, the kind of laugh a baddy in a cartoon would do. I reach forward and grab the back of her hair.

'Maybe your mental, anorexic sister gave it to me?' she says, acting like it doesn't hurt.

I automatically pull harder.

'Tell me, Sally. How did you get that letter.'

I pull more of her hair. I swear I won't let go until she tells me how she got it.

'Why should I tell you any—'

I twist the final twist before we both know the entire handful of hair is coming out.

'All right, all right. Let go, I'll tell you,' she says, before I give her a bald patch.

I release my hand. A few strands of her hair remain wrapped around my fingers. She reorganises herself in front of the mirror.

'Your gran's a bit thick, isn't she?' she says calmly.

'What?'

'Your gran. I went round to your house. I was going to warn you off Flo, tell you exactly how I feel about you stealing my best friend, but you weren't there. Next thing I know I'm sitting at your gran's dirty kitchen table eating crap biscuits and drinking tea that tasted like stale water. She was banging on about your aunty, what a special person she is, and about how she was out with you looking for a new house, like I cared. I got so bored I asked to go to the loo. When I saw your bedroom the temptation was too much, even for a person with as much self-control as me. I opened your bedside drawer and hey presto, the last six months played out on paper. The way you stole Flo from me right before my eyes, the entire lie on paper. Her notes to you were so pathetic. *I've never had a friend like you. I didn't know girls like you existed.* What are you, lezzers?'

'No, we are friends. *Proper* friends.'

'Ha, that's a joke. She's totally disillusioned by you. I read through all her drippy, soppy notes to you and I found the one you had written to Julian. Right in amongst her fantasy was your big fat lie.'

The idea of Sally reading those notes, being in my bedroom, in my house, talking to Nana is horrible. I feel totally invaded, and even though I have known her for all these years I'm still shocked by how evil she really is.

'So I took it. Something that beautiful can't go to waste. Finders keepers and all that.'

She goes to walk away but I pull her back towards me. I am possessed by such extreme anger that the whole thing feels like a dream. I drag her by her hair into a cubicle, push her head down into the toilet bowl, and flush.

'You did WHAT?'

Even Aunty Jo is struggling to see how I am going to get out of this one. We are in the kitchen cooking dinner that night and trying to keep our voices down so Nana and Pop don't hear us from the living room.

'I was so angry. I couldn't bring myself to punch her in the face so bog washing was the next best thing. Now everyone knows about me and Julian and Flo will never forgive me. I lost it, I totally lost it. And now Gem's mum is going to kill me for ruining the jeans, and everyone knows about how I stuffed loo roll in Flo's pants, and Flo will hate me for that as well, even though I was just trying to help,' I say, slightly hysterically.

'I'll call Gem's mum and explain about the jeans. You just focus on Flo,' Aunty Jo says, giving me a reassuring look.

The doorbell rings.

'Here, keep your eye on the rice and I'll get the door,' she says as she goes to the front door.

I hold a wooden spoon in my hand and stare at the

rice. A pan of chilli is bubbling next to it but I don't think I could mange even the smallest mouthful. Aunty Jo comes back in. Miss Anthony is with her.

'Turn the heat off for a minute, Renée. Miss Anthony needs to talk to us.' Aunty Jo pokes her head into the lounge. 'It's OK, Mum, it's someone for me.' She shuts the door behind her and joins Miss Anthony and I at the table. I brace myself for a good telling-off.

'What you did to Sally was very dangerous, Renée. People have been drowned that way,' Miss Anthony says with a very serious face.

I nod.

'Sally was wrong to write your personal letter on the blackboard, though. What she did was very cruel. That infringement of your personal feelings is understandably going to be very upsetting and I do appreciate that, but to push her head into a toilet and flush it really was a very extreme reaction.'

I nod again. Aunty Jo looks at me as if she still can't believe I did it.

'Sally's mother has made an official complaint to the school about the incident, and we have had to act accordingly,' says Miss Anthony. 'I am sorry to have to tell you this, Renée, but we have no choice but to suspend you until the exams start.'

'Is that completely necessary?' asks Aunty Jo, shocked.

'I'm afraid so. We can't be seen to have any sort of tolerance for this sort of behaviour. Do you understand that, Renée?'

226

I nod again.

'I want you to know that I don't take what Sally did to you and Flo lightly either. I believe that you were provoked and I have insisted to Miss Grut that she is also punished for her behaviour, and also suspended.'

'What about lessons? Won't Renée miss out on important work for her exams?' Aunty Jo asks.

Miss Anthony shakes her head. 'All the coursework is done now, and what with the Easter holidays she will only actually miss three weeks of school. If you study hard, Renée, there is no reason that when you come back next term everything won't have settled down and you can move on into your A levels with confidence. Does that sound OK?'

I nod again.

'OK, well, I'll leave you to it. I'll post a full timetable of your exams to you this week, but I am sure your first one is maths on the 21st of May. So I'll see you there, OK?'

I nod one final time and thank Miss Anthony. This could have been a lot more horrible if Miss Trunks was my form teacher. Aunty Jo sees her out. I turn the stove back on.

'Right, well, I suggest you take a plate of food upstairs and hide yourself in your bedroom until the morning, yes?' Aunty Jo says as she comes back in.

'Can't I start revising tomorrow?' I ask. My head feels battered after today.

'I don't mean to revise, I mean so you can get out of the way. I'm now going to have to explain to your grandpa that you shoved a girl's head down a toilet and that you are suspended from school. I don't think you want to be within reach of him when he finds out, do you?'

I leave my food and get up to my room as quick as I can. I get into bed and hide my head under the pillow. What a massive mess I've made now.

Flo

How is it possible to go from feeling so good to feeling so devastated that no matter how hard you try you can't even remember how it feels to be happy? I'm sure just a few months ago I thought my life was as close to perfect as it could be, considering what has happened to me and who I have to put up with. Renée was the reason for all of that; she helped me cope. The two of us were indestructible, or so I thought. Sally must have felt so smug when she found that letter, like all her Christmases had come at once.

I keep going over and over what the letter said. The night Renée walked me home after the party, the fact that she put loo roll in my knickers. I thought I had done that myself. Oh my God. We've told each other everything since then – she could have told me about that. I might even have laughed. Actually, what am I talking about? We haven't been telling each other anything at all. She had sex with my brother and never told me that. What other lies are there? I feel so stupid. How could I have trusted her, the class's biggest joker, known for having no real

228

friends and not taking anything seriously? Why did I ever think our friendship was any different?.

I hear the front door open and slam shut again. Julian is home. Over a week has passed since I found out about him and Renée and he still doesn't know that I know. I haven't been able to face it. I feel different now. I stand at the top of the stairs.

'Hey, Julian,' I say firmly.

'All right. Why you being weird?' he asks, continuing to walk through the house.

'Can't I say hello to my big brother without being called weird?'

'Guess not.'

He goes into the kitchen. I follow him. I imagine him and Renée in it kissing while I was with Abi in the lounge. It gives me goosebumps. I stand behind him.

'So, I know you shagged Renée.' I'm past being subtle now. No one else seems to be able to control themselves, so why should I?

He jumps up to sit on the work surface and crosses his arms. I can't tell if he looks nervous or proud.

'Oh yeah? Tell you, did she?'

'Don't you have enough girls your own age to seduce, rather than ruining my friendships?' I ask him.

'Girls are so overdramatic. Why does that have to ruin your friendship?'

'You don't get it, do you? She slept with my brother a few months after our dad died then lied to me about it. How the hell can I be friends with her after that?' I say.

Does he seriously not see what the problem is?

'No, Flo.' He is shouting now. It feels unnecessary. 'YOU don't get it, do you? I don't know how much more obvious I can make it to you. He wasn't *our* dad.'

My heart changes rhythm.

'What did you say?' I ask, a lump forming in my throat.

'I found out a few years ago when I heard them arguing about it. You were too young to understand it so we just carried on pretending, but everything was fucked after that. Mum doesn't know where my real dad is. All she knows is that "Dad" wasn't my dad,' he says, raising his eyebrows as if I should have known.

I fall backwards into a chair. It's just a lucky coincidence that it was there.

'Was he definitely my dad?' I ask, momentarily petrified.

'Of course he was. You were almost the same person.'

How many blows can one person take before they are allowed to officially declare themselves destroyed? I've heard of people being winded by physical impact, but I am getting it from shock. For once Julian doesn't storm out of the room just because I'm in it. He continues to make himself a sandwich and even offers to make me one too. I don't accept it. I don't think my mouth would remember how to chew. He seems relieved to have finally got that off his chest. Good for him. I feel like a helicopter just landed on my head. I rest my chin on my hand and force myself to breathe.

The doorbell rings. I get it.

'Mr Du Putron, what are you –' I begin, very surprised to see him.

230

'Where is he?' he asks rudely.

I have always been scared of Sally's dad, but as an unexpected visitor at your house he is even more menacing.

'Sorry, who? Dad? Did Sally not tell you?'

'No, not your father, your brother. Your dirty bastard brother. Where is he?'

A plate clanks in the kitchen and Mr Du Putron pushes me aside as he storms through my house. I close the door, and by the time I get to the kitchen he is on top of Julian on the kitchen table and is punching him. I don't know what to do.

'Mr Du Putron, stop it!' I try to get close to them but the energy coming off him is like a barrier. 'What's going on?' I shout pointlessly.

'You dirty bastard. You put your filthy hands on my daughter and now she's pregnant. I'll kill you!' spits Sally's dad.

His words impact my brain as hard as Mr Du Putron's fists hit my brother's face. Sally is pregnant by Julian? What?

I watch him as he continues to hit Julian. A part of me knows I should stop him but the rest of me wants to see my brother get demolished. Eventually Julian manages to shove Mr Du Putron away, but he bangs his head on the table as he falls to the floor. Mr Du Putron lies there, panting heavily, then he gets to his feet, tells Julian he will pay for what he has done, and leaves.

I feel the rest of my world come crashing down around me.

'You could leave all your winter clothes here and get them when you come back?' I say to Nell as I watch her pull the clothes out of her cupboard.

'I'm not coming back, Renée,' she tells me in her usual cold tone.

'I just think you should keep an open mind about this. If you get your hopes up too much and it doesn't work out then you will be so disappointed,' I say, in an attempt to be sisterly.

'Stop trying to bring me down, will you? Can't you see that for the first time in years I am actually looking forward to something?' Nell snaps.

I feel like I don't know her at all. I feel so hated by her, and so unable to make it better. What chance do we ever have of becoming close if she lives in Spain?

'I'm going to miss you,' I say as I sit on the edge of my bed and cry. She stops packing and looks at me. Her hard face softens, taking me by surprise.

'I think we both have to change, don't you? I know I'm the psycho out of the two of us, but you can't carry on being the way you are either,' Nell says, sounding so grown-up.

I'm not quite sure what part of me she is talking about, but I nod. I don't know how I always get things so wrong. I don't mean to.

'Here, I'll help you with that.' I get up and carry her case downstairs. Nana, Pop and Aunty Jo are all waiting in the drive.

232

'Your grandpa is going to take you to the airport. I don't think I could cope with saying goodbye there,' says Nana, her hair done perfectly. She wraps her arms around Nell, and cries the most honest tears she has cried in years.

'Come on, and one for your favourite aunty too,' says Aunty Jo. She gives her a huge squeeze and kisses her head. 'You can always come back, OK?'

Nell nods.

I stand waiting for my cuddle, I don't know why I think I'll get one but I hope it so much. My breath is loud and jerky. I explode with grief when Nell gets straight into the car without saying goodbye to me. I still don't know what I did to make her so mad at me. Pop drives her away, and I sob out eight years of agony into Aunty Jo's shoulder. As she leads me back into the house, I hear Nell's voice.

'Renée?'

Pop's car has stopped halfway down the hill. Nell is standing next to it. After a short pause we run so fast that we smack into each other so hard it should hurt. We squeeze so tight that I don't think I can ever let her go, our wet cheeks squashed together in a moment that we both thought would never happen, but need so much.

'I'm sorry,' she says.

'I'm sorry too.'

'Come on, Nell. You will miss your flight,' says Aunty Jo as she gently pulls us apart and guides her back to the car. I watch as Pop drives her away. She looks back at me until they are totally out of sight. I have no idea when I will see my sister again.

233

11
Working Out the Answers

Flo

The school hall feels so different – institutional, stark, unwelcoming. I'm used to it being the place where four hundred of us group together every morning and sing hymns, listen to readings and laugh about all the cat hair stuck to Miss Grut's clothes, but today it is an exam hall and the atmosphere is serious. There are five perfectly straight rows of small desks around two metres apart. Mine is three from the back, Sally's is in front of me to the left, Renée must be somewhere behind me. I daren't turn around to look. The three of us being in the same room since *that* morning is another distraction from my first GCSE exam that I really don't need.

I look at Sally. Her hair is messier than usual. Since Miss Anthony announced that the exam had begun she's been writing furiously. Something tells me she has more to prove than usual.

I think about Dad, how proud he would be of me if I do well. How if I pass my exams I can get away from all this – go to university, find new friends, live on my own, get a job and buy my own clothes and make something of my life. I get stuck in. I can do this. I can get good grades.

About half an hour in Miss Anthony gets up and walks up and down each of the rows. She's wearing a pink flowery skirt with a pale pink blouse and soft-soled shoes. I wonder if she's been told to wear soft-soled shoes so the sound of her feet doesn't distract us. As she gets to me her eyes glance over my work and I feel a sudden fear that the answers I have given are wrong. Without thinking I shield them from her view with my arm. The fear of failing this exam brings on a controllable but nauseating panic attack. My breath gets harder to catch, and I'm about to get up, leave school, leave the exams. I can't do this. Just as I prepare to run out a paper aeroplane skims the side of my face and lands on my exam paper.

I look at it then flip my head from side to side to see if anyone saw. This could fail me my GCSE. How can Renée do this? Miss Anthony is seconds away from looping round the bottom of the row and walking back up towards me again. If she sees the note it's game over. I snatch it from in front of me and stuff it into my bra. Miss Anthony sees the final stage of this move so I have to causally act like my nipple is itchy. She looks away quickly. I think I got away with it. Through my rage I carry on with my maths exam. I do not and will not acknowledge Renée. I don't want to be manipulated any more.

235

At the end we have to leave the hall row by row in total silence. I don't want to see anyone, so I keep my head down and walk as quickly as I can out of the school. But obviously not quickly enough.

'Flo, Flo. Wait.'

It's Sally. She's chasing me.

'Flo, WAIT FOR ME!'

Whatever part of my brain it was that she trained to obey her responds and I stop. She is in front of me. Her face looks fatter.

'You can't walk away from me, Flo. Not any more,' Sally warns me.

'What do you mean, not any more?'

'Now I am,' she whispers, 'pregnant with your brother's baby.'

The words 'half-brother' fly into my mouth, but I choose not to say them.

'Oh yes, that. Your dad did mention that,' I say, obviously fuming about his turning up to my house and punching Julian's lights out in our kitchen.

For once she doesn't have an answer. Instead I see a flicker of something vulnerable in her eyes. Guilt, maybe. It's hard to tell with her.

'Mum was worried the police would arrest Dad,' she says, sheepishly.

'You're not even sixteen, Sally. Neither was Renée. Julian wants to keep this as quiet as possible. So quiet that he's left Guernsey. He just packed up and went. Who knows what he is thinking.'

'What do you mean, left Guernsey? When will he be back? He can't just leave!' Sally says, looking panicked.

'Yeah, well, he has. So I guess that tells us what kind of person he really is, doesn't it? And as for you, Jesus, Sally! You went to all of that effort to expose Renée when all the while you were doing the same thing. You are pregnant with my brother's baby. How could you do that?'

'Don't blame me! It's not my fault he doesn't use condoms, is it? And stop being so mean to me, I . . .' There's that look again. That vulnerability. It isn't enough to force an apology out of her, but it's enough to make me realise that Sally is frightened. 'My dad is really mad, Flo. Really, really mad.'

I imagine the baby in her tummy. I want to hate it, I want to hate her, but even if Julian is only my half-brother, somewhere down the line that baby is a part of me. I already feel sorry for it, that Sally is its mother, that Julian is its dad. What chance does it have? Maybe I am its only chance. NO. I have to ignore these feelings. This isn't my problem. Whatever mess she has got herself into it is hers to sort out. I have enough to deal with.

'Well, then, you should have controlled yourself. I don't want anything to do with you, Sally. I didn't before and I certainly don't now. You're on your own.' I walk away.

'But Flo, you're my best friend!'

I don't look back.

Sitting on my bed later that night I should be revising for my English literature exam in the morning, but the note

237

that Renée threw at me is in my rucksack and I swear I can hear it whispering my name. 'I miss you' is written on its left wing; the front is weighted down with a small ball of blue tac. What could it possibly say to make any of this better? The word sorry doesn't even begin to cover it. Then it strikes me. What if she is pregnant too? I start to unfold it. I'm nervous, angry, and determined not to forgive her, no matter what it says.

Dear Flo

I adjust my pillow so that I am comfortable. I take a sip of tea, a deep breath, and continue to read.

Sorry I threw this at you in an exam. I know that will have made you mad but I also knew you wouldn't take it from me if I tried to give it to you. My life has changed so much since we last spoke, but even though all the things that were wrong before I met you are better, I am finding not seeing or talking to you so hard.

I know I'm always getting told off at school for messing around, and by Pop for whatever reason he can think of to have a go at me, and I know it's usually my fault. But the way I feel about you being angry with me is different. I can't handle it.

I was going to tell you everything. Lying was driving me crazy and I wanted to be honest. I am so sorry I had sex with Julian. I thought I loved him but obviously I didn't, I just got sucked in. If it's any consolation, after that night in his car he never spoke to me again and left me feeling so horrible about myself that if you think I haven't suffered like you have then you are wrong. I have hated myself more than I think you could ever hate me, so please don't think I got off lightly.

What's worse out of all of this is that I have lost you, the one true friend I've ever had. You are the best person I have ever known and I miss you every day. What makes it even worse is that you're just a few miles away but the only reason I can't see you is because you don't want to see me. Nothing I ever do will ever make me feel as guilty or as heartbroken as that makes me feel.

Margaret told me about Sally and Julian. If I'm honest I'm not surprised. I know I am not one to talk but she got what she deserved. Of all the condoms to break, though, right?

I love you. I want you to be my friend again. I don't know if people forgive for things like this, but if there is any part of you that ever wants to go back to how things were, then I am all yours.

R x

I wipe a stream of tears from my cheek and sit holding the letter for a few minutes before rolling it into a ball and throwing it into the bin. I can't forgive her, and I won't.

The front door slams shut. Mum is home.

Fred is with her. His words of comfort are hard to hear under the sound of her wailing.

I hear a bottle smash and then a thud. Fred tells her to pull herself together. She screams at him to leave her alone and he leaves, slamming the front door behind him. I swear that door is going to fall off its hinges soon.

I make my way downstairs. Mum is on her hands and knees in the kitchen sweeping up the broken glass with a dustpan and brush. She looks up at me. She looks so tired.

'What are you doing? I need to be on my own,' she says wearily.

'Have you heard from Julian? Where did he go?' I ask, ignoring her need for space.

'Why do you care?'

'Mum, can you stop hating me for just one moment? I just want to know where he went.'

She sits back onto her feet and takes a breath to calm herself down.

'He's in London. He's going to try to get a job in the City, he thinks, but for now he has a part-time job in a garage. I hope your little friend is proud of herself.'

'Julian having sex with my friends is not my fault, and I don't like it any more than you do, OK?'

For once she doesn't come back at me with something scathing.

'Make me a cup of tea, will you. I'm desperate.' Mum sits at the kitchen table. She exhales a few long breaths and takes off her shoes, allowing herself to relax.

I remove the tea bag from the mug, throw it in the bin,

pass her the mug and say, 'Just before Mr Du Putron arrived, Julian told me that Dad wasn't really his dad. Is that true?'

The cup freezes just as it gets to her lips and her eyes rest on my face. I am standing over her, waiting for the answer.

'Flo, can't you see I am tired?'

'You're tired? I'm tired of being lied to and I have the right to know this, at least. Was Dad Julian's dad or not?'

She takes a loud slurp of tea, lights a cigarette and then starts to speak.

'No. No, he wasn't. OK? He wasn't Julian's dad.'

I feel my brain jolt forward, pushing tears towards my eyes, but somehow I manage to hold them back.

'Well, then who was his dad?'

'Someone I really loved,' Mum says, her eyes softening.

'What do you mean, really loved? Didn't you really love Dad?'

'Not like I loved him, no. I had an affair when your father and I were first together. His name was David. I thought we would end up together, but his wife found out and left him over it and somehow that was my fault. He quit his job here and left the island, leaving me to deal with the mess we had made. Part of that was the baby I was carrying, his baby. I was frightened and heartbroken, and your dad, well, he was just willing to carry on like nothing had happened. So that's what we did, we lived a lie for all those years.'

She takes a long drag on her cigarette and forces a guilty smile.

241

'Why didn't you marry David if you loved him so much?' I ask, finally starting to understand something about my mother.

'Because he wasn't brave enough to face up to any of it. He was a coward. So many men are. You will see that one day. I've always wanted to tell you, but the longer you leave something like that, the harder it gets. I *am* sorry. Flo.' Mum seems to be about to reach out for my hand, but changes her mind at the last minute.

'Do you ever speak to him now?' I ask, not quite managing to process her apology.

'No, I never heard from him again. He never once got in touch to ask about the baby. But if he turned up tomorrow, I'd forgive him,' Mum says frankly.

'But what he did was awful. He left his wife, then left you and Julian. How could you ever forgive him for any of that?' I ask, getting confused.

'Because there are some people in life that you have to forgive, no matter what they do. Because without them you're nothing. You have no choice,' Mum says, stubbing out her cigarette. She blows out until all of the smoke has left her lungs and says, 'You can't escape it when you love someone. It becomes a part of who you are. If you're lucky enough to stop loving someone who doesn't love you then fine, but if you can't then it's the worst pain a person can feel. And that's the pain that I've lived with all these years. He took a part of me with him when he left and I never got it back.'

Mum gets up and moves into the living room to lie on

the sofa. I pour myself a glass of water and go back up to my room. I take Renée's letter out of the bin, and read it another five times before I finally fall asleep.

Renée

I watch the clock. Has it broken? No, it's moving, just so slowly. The sound of everyone else's pens scratching on their exam papers is almost deafening. I don't seem to know anything. How do I not know anything? I never even skived geography. What was I doing in all of those lessons that means I didn't learn any of this stuff? When Miss Trunks finally says the time is up, I can't wait to get outside.

'Hi, guys,' I say as I walk up to Charlotte, Bethan and Nancy. 'Shall we go down to the hockey pitch and rub out the white lines on the grass?'

'Sorry, Renée. We are going up to the library to revise for the French exam this afternoon. You can come if you like?' says Charlotte, looking a bit worried about me.

'No, I'm cool. I've got stuff to do. Good luck.'

I watch them walk away. They used to be so much fun. Everyone has got so serious lately.

'Margaret,' I shout as I see her outside the toilets. 'Let's go have a fag?'

'Sorry, Renée. I need to stay here and go over my French vocabulary. I think I want to do French for A level,' she says with excitement.

'Come on, Margaret. We can go to the bike sheds and swap everyone's wheels around?'

'Sorry, Renée. I want to do well. I need to pass my GCSEs.' She turns and walks towards the library. I think better of calling after her.

As I walk out of school I see Carla and Gem sitting on the grass, textbooks out. It looks like Gem is testing Carla on her French. They look up and wave. I smile back and keep walking like I actually have somewhere to go.

I walk down the hill towards town. I see boys starting to fill the pavement in front of me as they pile out of their school in their lunch break. Then I see Lawrence, on his own as usual, holding a bottle of Coke and a brown paper sandwich bag. He sees me through the crowd and starts to walk away. I feel like I have nothing to lose.

'Lawrence, Lawrence!' I call after him. All the other boys are laughing at me because he won't turn around. I run to catch up with him and put my hand on his shoulder. 'Lawrence, please talk to me.'

'Why would I want to talk to you?' he says, his face still so angry, like no time has passed at all. 'Need some attention, do you? On your terms, obviously. Everyone else has dumped you so now you are running back to me thinking I'll be stupid enough to forgive you?'

'Did you hear about what happened with Flo's brother?' I ask, feeling that I need to know this before I say anything else.

'There isn't anyone under the age of twenty-five on the

244

entire island that doesn't know about you and Flo's brother. You put out pretty quickly for him, didn't you? The guys in my year take the piss out of me every day because you didn't want to lose your virginity to me but you couldn't wait to lose it to him. Thanks for that.'

I hadn't thought about Lawrence getting a hard time over this too. I feel even worse. He carries on walking away from me.

'I'm sorry,' I shout after him. 'I'm sorry for making you feel stupid for having feelings for me, and I'm sorry for leading you on. I'm sorry if I was mean to you, and I'm sorry for what happened with Julian and that you got shit for it too. I wish it had never happened.'

He turns and goes to speak but stops himself. I stand in front of him feeling so pitiful it's almost painful. I think he starts to feel sorry for me. He gets out some fags and offers me one. I wait for him to take it first so he can light it in his mouth, but he doesn't.

'Friends don't do that kind of thing, do they?' he says, offering me a peace-making smile.

'No, friends don't,' I agree.

I take the fag and light it myself. He gives me half of his sandwich and we walk into town to get chips. I tell him everything, and he doesn't tell me he loves me.

12

When All Else Fails

Renée

'Today's the day,' says Aunty Jo, as we unpack more of her clothes that have been sent from London. 'What time do you get your results?'

'I need to be at school for 11 a.m.,' I say, as I hang a dress up in her wardrobe. My hands are visibly shaking.

Aunty Jo goes to the sofa and pats the seat next to her. 'Come here,' she says. 'I was useless at school, and my life has been OK. I've travelled the world, owned businesses and now look, I am renting a nice house on a beautiful island and I have my brilliant niece living with me. Life turned out OK for me, didn't it? Whatever happens today doesn't mean the rest of your life is defined by it, OK?'

'OK,' I say, still unsure.

'Go on, why don't you walk up to school now? Go the long way, clear your head. Get ready for a nice surprise.

246

I'm sure you haven't done as badly as you think. Today might end up being a good day. Imagine that.' She smiles.

I leave the house and walk towards school. It's only ten thirty, so rather than hurry I go down into the Sunken Gardens to smoke. The last time I was here it was pelting with rain and freezing cold, Flo and I were hugging and laughing and drawing on the wall. How did that all go so wrong? I look at the wall. *Renée ♥ Flo* is still there as if it was written yesterday. My guilt feels just as fresh.

Every day throughout the exams I hoped to find a paper aeroplane in my school bag, but I never did. I don't even know if she read my letter – maybe she just threw it away. I wouldn't blame her, I guess. I stub my fag out onto my name and head up to Tudor Falls. I need to get these results over and done with.

As I approach the school I can see that almost my entire class is already there. Carla and Gem are jumping up and down in the car park screaming 'Eight A*! OH MY GOD!' I walk past them. Inside, Margaret comes straight over.

'I passed five, PHEW. Maths, English, science, drama and French. I guess I could be a French scientist when I grow up then?' She scuttles off, laughing at herself. Next I see Charlotte and Bethan, both excited to have got six GCSEs each. I congratulate them and keep walking towards the table where the envelopes with our names on are laid out. I scan them. Flo's has already gone, so has Sally's. I pick up my envelope and take it outside, finding a bench at the edge of the playground. I open the envelope.

I've passed. I have passed everything. An A for drama, Bs for both English, C for maths and five little 'a's for everything else. I'm shocked, amazed in fact. Why had I been so frightened? Of course I would pass my . . . and then I realise. I couldn't even get As for the subjects I took – I was in the lower set for all of them. I look again at the results. Those five little italic 'a's are actually 'd's. I've failed everything but four. I've failed. I don't have enough GCSEs to stay at Tudor Falls.

Confusion comes first, then shock, then I level out on fear. What am I going to do? I'm so embarrassed. Girls all around me are screaming with joy over their results, hugging each other, hugging their parents, laughing and jumping up and down. And here is me, alone in my moment, feeling instantly like a trespasser at Tudor Falls. How could I have been so stupid? How have I failed all but four? No one fails all but four. I'll have to go to the grammar school, no one there will know me, Flo will forget about me and I'll never get her back. I'll have to tell all those new people that my mum died when I was seven, and they'll all ask me about it, and no one will know anything about me, and I'll have to start all over again and I can't do that. That's even worse than coming back here next term and facing everyone after what I did to Flo.

I walk aimlessly back into the school and towards the toilets. Margaret runs after me and asks me how I did. I pass her my results form, then grab it back and keep on going.

'You failed?' she whispers as she comes after me. I think this is the first time I've ever seen her so effortlessly control the volume of her voice.

'Yeah, I've failed. I am officially the most stupid person in our year,' I say, very matter of fact.

'So you're leaving Tudor Falls?'

'Looks like it,' I say, coldly.

'I'll miss you,' she says.

A part of me wants to shove her aside and continue into the toilets, where I can crack on with having my breakdown, but she looks so upset.

'You're my best friend,' she says, her eyes now fixed on the floor.

I've never thought about myself as important to Margaret before, but of course I am. We've been partners in class for five years. The two of us had no one else so we stuck together. A wave of guilt comes over me as I think about her in the sixth form sitting on her own and feeling lonely.

'I'll miss you too,' I tell her, as I put my arms around her, realising that this is the first act of affection we have ever shared.

'You'll make new friends at the grammar and forget about me. I know that,' she says quietly.

I should reassure her but I can't lie. Mean as it sounds, I think it's OK to be honest about who people are in your life. It saves you or them being disappointed if you can't keep up the lie. Realising that I would never be as

249

important to Carla and Gem as they are to each other was one of the biggest revelations I could have had. I don't want to lead Margaret on. I know that our friendship won't go beyond Tudor Falls. We're different kinds of people.

'Go on, go home and tell your mum how well you did. I'll see you around, yeah?' I say.

She wipes her eyes and walks away. As I watch her, Miss Anthony calls me.

'Come in here, Renée. Come on.' She gestures for me to go into Room Six.

I sit at my old desk, she sits at Flo's. I take this as my cue to start crying.

'I heard about your results,' says Miss Anthony gently. 'There are still lots of options for you, Renée. You mustn't feel like this is the end of your education. The grammar school could be good for you. There are more non-academic subjects, and a change might be just what you need.'

I stare aimlessly at the blackboard, remembering my life plastered all over it.

'Renée, how are you feeling?'

I turn to Miss Anthony. Her face is full of pity for me. Fair enough. I am a loser on every level.

'I feel like a waste of space. Like my whole life has been building up to the moment I failed. Like I don't have the energy to make up for what I've done, or to start again, or for anything. I feel like I want to be someone else.'

Miss Anthony moves to Margaret's old seat and puts her arm around me.

250

'You're not the tough little cookie everyone thinks you are, are you?'

As much as it pains me to do so, I shake my head.

'Will your family be OK with your results? Would you like me to talk to them?'

'No, it will be fine. Things at home are fine.' It is nice to be able to say that, without it being a lie.

When I eventually summon the courage to leave Room Six I go into the toilets and splash my face with cold water. I stare at my reflection in the mirror. I never thought my time here would end so dismally. School was always the place I was happiest. This wasn't supposed to happen.

When I get down into the foyer everyone has gone. The table that had our results on is cleared, and the caretaker is jingling his keys, obviously keen to lock up and get on with his summer holiday.

'Bye, Mr Blake,' I shout to him. He doesn't hear me as he disappears into his office.

I carry on out. As I walk across the playground I remember the games of tag we played at break, the time I fell over and scraped my knee – I still have the scar. The time Margaret convinced herself there was a man in the bushes and the entire school got sent inside only to discover the gardener was in there digging up a tree. It all seems like so long ago already.

As I walk towards the school gate I see a silhouette that makes my heart jump. I get closer, preparing myself to be hammered further into the ground.

251

Flo

When I see Renée coming towards me I don't know where to look. Should I watch her as she walks or look away and act surprised when she gets to me? Neither. I should be bold. I start walking towards her. We stop and stand face to face. Tudor Falls is behind her, watching us to see what happens next.

'I saw Margaret. She told me about your results. She looked as upset as you do,' I say, quite shocked by how pale she is.

'I bet you think I'm even more of a loser now, don't you?' she asks, not looking at me.

'I couldn't think you were more of a loser,' I say.

She nods and keeps her head down.

'How did you do?' she asks me after a short pause.

'I passed everything. Four As, three Bs, two Cs. I did well,' I say, trying not to look too happy about it.

'That's great. I'm really pleased for you. I, on other the other hand, have ruined my life.'

'What are you going to do? Grammar school? A job?' I ask, trying to move the conversation along.

'Grammar school, I guess, if they'll have me. I can't stay here anyway. At least you'll be rid of me. I'm sure you're pleased about that. I don't blame you.'

'Actually I –' I'm cut off by the sound of a car rolling to a standstill behind me. I hear a door shut, then another. Renée looks angry. I turn around. It's Sally and her mum.

'Florence,' says Mrs Du Putron as she pushes Sally by the elbow towards me. 'Sally has something she needs to tell you, don't you, Sally?'

Sally folds her arms. She huffs and tuts in her usual style, then after a few seconds her entire face changes, and she starts to sob. Renée and I share a bemused look. This is a first.

'I'm sorry, Flo. I'm sorry for what I've done,' blubs Sally.

I'm confused. First Sally cries and then she says sorry? Is this really happening?

'Come on, Sally. Tell Florence why you are sorry,' urges her mother.

Renée steps forward and stands next to me. Sally sniffs in a nose full of snot and starts to speak. She is spitting and spluttering all over the place.

'I never slept with Julian. He isn't the father of my baby. I didn't mean for it to get so out of hand. I didn't know Dad would beat him up and that he would leave Guernsey.'

The atmosphere feels as pregnant as her belly.

'What did you say?' asks Renée, her head thrust forward, her bottom lip hanging low.

'I said that I never slept with Julian. I made it up. He isn't the father of my baby,' repeats Sally, dropping her head.

'Well, who is the father then?' asks Renée. More capable of words than me.

'Phil.'

'Who's Phil?' asks Renée, getting annoyed.

'Oh my God, the twenty-seven-year-old from your dad's work?' I say, horrified. 'You actually had sex with him? Did your dad beat him up as well?'

'My husband deeply regrets what he did to your brother, Flo. He isn't one for controlling himself when he gets upset,' said Mrs Du Putron.

'Please forgive me, Flo. The school have said that I can come back next term and study from home when the baby comes. We can still be best friends, and we can sit next to each other when I come in, can't we?' begs Sally.

I take a moment to examine her face. A face that has instilled such fear into me for so long. A face that has disempowered me, put me down, hurt my feelings and demoralised me over and over again. I have no pity for her at all. I could quite happily never see her ever again.

'Actually no,' I say. 'I won't be at Tudor Falls next year. I'm going to the grammar school.'

'You're what?' asks Renée, stunned.

'Yup. Mum has kindly refused to fork out for my Tudor Falls school fees any more so I'm coming to the grammar school too,' I say, offering Renée a forgiving smile.

'What do you mean, "too"?' asks Sally, as her tears dry up and she starts to resemble the Sally we all know and hate.

'Me and Renée. We're going together. Isn't that right, Renée?'

'That's, right,' she says, still confused but smiling too.

I walk closer to Sally. I take a good look at her face. I hope it's the last time I ever see it. 'Because *we* are best friends,' I say, looking her right in the eye. 'Good luck with motherhood. I'm off to live my life.'

As Sally watches us, speechless, her face pulsing from the shock, I link my arm through Renée's and we walk away. Leaving a lifetime of memories behind us, my best friend and I leave Tudor Falls for the very last time.

Epilogue
October 1995

Renée

'I'm coming!' I shout out of the window as Aunty Jo beeps her horn for the fifth time.

I shove the last of my books into my bag, zip it up and run down the stairs. After slamming the front door behind me I mouth 'Sorry' at Aunty Jo as the house rattles from the force of it.

'Honestly, Renée. If you are ever on time for school it will be a miracle,' she says, driving away from the house.

I turn the radio on and we sing along to 'Country House' by Blur. We make each other laugh by doing silly voices on the word 'countrrryyyyyy'.

'OK, quickly this morning,' she tells me as we pull up at Flo's house. I get out of the car and run up the drive. I knock once then go in.

'Morning!' I shout through the hallway.

'Bloody hell, Renée, do you have to shout?' says Flo's mum as she comes out of the kitchen.

'Sorry, Mrs Parrot. Morning,' I whisper.

She rolls her eyes.

'Hey,' says Flo as she comes down the stairs. She looks cool in a tightish blue cardigan and a navy checked skirt, thick tights and black shoes. I still can't get over how good it is not having to wear uniforms. Just one of the perks of being a sixth former at the grammar school. That, and boys.

'Here you go, girls. One of these each,' says Flo's mum, offering us a plate with two slices of toast and Nutella on it.

'Bye, Mum,' says Flo. 'Are you still OK to pick me up after hockey tonight?'

'Yes, but don't take ages in the changing room this time. I get stuck talking to the other mums when you do that and I have about as much in common with them as I do interest in hockey.'

'I won't.'

HONK HONK.

'Bye, Mrs Parrot,' I say, getting Aunty Jo's hint loud and clear.

From the back seat I ask Flo to turn up the music. It's 'Without You' by Mariah Carey. The three of us sing it (badly) at the top of our lungs. As we pull up to the school entrance other pupils look at us like we are idiots, but we don't care.

'I think Marcus Holmes is going to ask you out today,' I say to Flo as we get out of the car.

'No way! He fancies Vanessa Finton. It's so obvious,' she says, brushing it off like she always does when I say things like this.

'When are you ever going to get a bloody boyfriend?' I tease, pinching her on the arm.

'When are you going to think about anything other than food or boys?' she jokes back.

'Come on, I'll race you to the common room,' I say. 'Last one there buys chips at lunch.'

We both start to run.

'BYE THEN?' shouts Aunty Jo after us. We hear her but the stakes are too high to turn back. Along the corridor our new headmaster, Mr Bailey, shouts at us to stop running. Our feet stop before our bodies so we land in a giggling heap on the floor.

'Renée and Flo, how many times do I have to tell you that the school corridors are not a running track?' he says, standing over us.

We pick ourselves up and try to stop laughing.

'Sorry, Mr Bailey,' we proclaim in unison.

'I think he fancies you,' I say as he disappears around the corner.

'OH, SHUT UP!' Flo yells, thumping me on the arm.

We walk calmly to the common room, giggling all the way.

Acknowledgements

Thank you Emily Thomas, for calling me out of the blue and making my lifelong dream of writing fiction into a reality. And for being the kind of editor who says, 'It's a bit far, I love it', rather than pulling me back. And for making me feel constantly encouraged and confident and like I could actually do this. I'm looking forward to doing it all over again.

Thank you to Georgia Murray for the meticulous line editing, and all at Hot Key Books for making being published an exciting, inspiring and fun experience. A brilliant team from marketing to editing. I'm very proud to be in the line-up with such a hot new publisher.

Adrian Sington, my literary agent, who has been there from the first time I said 'I want to write books' and thus seen me through to now. What fun the future holds.

Laura Hill, Alex Crump and Claire Morgan at Independent for being in control of my life and just being generally awesome. Alex, I miss you.

Laura Symons and Laura Hopps at Premier for pulling out the stops on the PR. I think people got the message!

John Di Garis for my fabulous cover photo and my cousin Elise Rix and her lovely friend Kerry Bowden for being Renée and Flo. Thanks to Jet Purdie at Hot Key Books for being patient and working with the image to create a fabulous jacket for *Paper Aeroplanes*. I love it.

Thank you Caroline Flack for the quote for the cover, and for being a great friend and someone I can rely on to be ridiculous with. Same goes for you Jo Elvin of *Glamour* magazine. Thank you, thank you.

Thank you to Andrew Anthonio and all at Mayfair Associates for making me feel endlessly secure and supported. We got through the bad times, now let the good times roll.

All the girls of Ladies College in the 90s. Most of you inspired this in some way. Special shout out to Janet Unit, Lucy Guilbert and Diana Kennedy for the stories and trips down memory lane. I hope this makes you smile.

Thanks to Lilu . . . my cat, my muse. (That's right, I thanked my cat.) Who disappeared and devastated me, then came home the day I finished the last word of this book. Oddly found on the doorstep of one of my favourite authors, Lionel Shriver, which I translate as her giving me a sign that this whole writing a book thing was a good idea. Better also give a shout out to our dog, Potato. Because he is just the best little guy, and those extra heartbeats when I write make all the difference to me. (Yup, I thanked my dog as well.)

My most amazing friends Louise and Carrie for being the inspiration to this story. It is the way you guys make me feel that gave me the inspiration to write 70,000 words about friendship.

And my wonderful husband who high-fived me every time I finished a chapter. Those little moments of support are what get you through a daunting task like writing a book. Thank you for the mini celebrations every time I achieved something tiny and thank you for letting me bang on about two teenage girls who I hope you now understand. You're nice and I like what happened.

My family, past and present.

And then I am going to thank Twitter, because I am modern. Without Twitter all those hours alone would have been spent ACTUALLY working and this book would have been finished a year ago. So thanks a lot Twitter, thanks a lot!

Dawn O'Porter

Dawn O'Porter is a broadcaster and print journalist who lives in London with her husband Chris, cat Lilu and dog Potato. She has made documentaries about all sorts of things, including polygamy, childbirth, geishas, body image, breast cancer and even the movie Dirty Dancing.

Dawn has written for various UK newspapers and magazines including *Grazia* and *Stylist*. Although Dawn lives in London she spends a lot of time in LA and travels a lot. You may have seen her dragging two huge pink suitcases with broken wheels and her Siamese cat Lilu in a box through airports. At some point she plans to get new suitcases – the cat, however, has a few years left in her yet.

PAPER AEROPLANES is Dawn's first novel.

Follow Dawn at www.dawnporter.net or on Twitter: @hotpatooties